A Cat for All Seasons

by R. M. Kinder

LiquidAmber Publishing

Published by LiquidAmber
Henderson, Nevada

9 8 7 6 5 4 3 2 1

R. M. Kinder

A Cat for All Seasons

ISBN-13: 978-0-9895034-3-3

Although this is a work of fiction, the domestic
animal interactions are based on real events.

For the creatures dear to our hearts

CHAPTERS

Zeno's Beginning

He was born at the end of a mild July, with enough rain to keep the grass green and thick, and to keep the trees leafy above and cool and shady beneath. He didn't think in terms of trees or shade. He was a kitten, one of six. What he felt one can only surmise, but given the way he mewled and leaned into the others and squirmed as if they were one creature, he knew pleasure and contentment, and hunger, and maybe frustration. But all kittens squirm and mewl and then fall asleep. The mother, who was a good mother, purred and made another sound the kittens heard and humans could hear, too, if they listened closely and gained cues from the subtle quickening of the kittens. They would know that something was being transmitted. Love. Encouragement. Longing.

This last because the mother occasionally reached out and curled her paw and arm over, and sometimes the other paw and arm under, and pulled an armful of kittens to her as if she would hug them into her heart. They were loved.

The white one is the kitten we follow. He was the only white one, and very fragile—meaning that he was thin—and his skin seemed to be pearly beneath the white hair, so a kind of glow came from him. His nose was pink. At first his eyes were the most startling blue, and quizzical, as if he had a million questions. His mother had enough milk for all the babies and so he thrived as much as they all did.

When the kittens were six weeks old, the woman took them to the Farmers Market on Saturday, and again mid-week. People would stop and admire and adore the kittens and some were adopted. On the third visit to Farmers Market, the last kitten besides the white one was taken. The white one sensed a loss, and missed the wrapping of warmth that he remembered, a soft pile of family, and sounds and smells. All that was weaker now. When the couple returned to the farm, and he was in a box in the seat of the truck, and the truck bounced and jarred him, he felt too much space around him. He wanted a buffer and climbed out and got into the woman's lap. She didn't make him move. He mewled, and in a few minutes settled down on her lap and slept, despite the jarring. He dreamed, very likely, though the sights and sounds aren't truly known. Possibly he saw his small family individually and all together or just felt himself wrapped in a strengthening, comforting sleep.

"I can see why no one wants him," the woman told her husband. She had given the white kitten a saucer of canned milk. He lapped a little, then walked to the door. The screen door had a wide board at the bottom, and the white kitten could see over it if he pulled himself straight. He did that. "He's too serious," she continued. "Intense, really." Later, when she and her husband had eaten dinner and were watching news on the television, the kitten crawled up her leg and into her lap. In a few moments, she sneezed, and her husband glanced over.

"There you go," he said. "You're allergic to them, no matter the color."

She nodded, and carried the white kitten outside, holding him close but lightly to her abdomen. She couldn't find his mother, and so put the kitten in a cat-carry. It was made to keep a little creature comfortable if it were hurt and had to be taken to the animal shelter or to a veterinarian.   Many soft, clean rags covered the bottom. The woman added a shallow metal bowl with a sandbag base and put a bit of water in it.

"We'll find you a place," she said. He seemed so little alone, and so pale, and his blue eyes held hers. He stretched forward, placing one paw down and then the other and lowering his head almost in a bow. She had seen big cats do this, showing they weren't afraid, they were perfectly at ease. It was like yawning with the body. Then he sat back, regally, and looked at her.

He was so tiny. He needed to stay with her.

"You'd have to live outside," she said. "I don't think you're strong enough."

He mewled for quite a while. He heard a hoot owl and went silent. He didn't know about owls. Or vultures. He slept and occasionally made a sad sound that most creatures recognize—a baby alone.

In the deepest part of the night, while the man and woman were sleeping soundly, something heavy came onto the porch and the scent of it woke the kitten. He saw it and though it was from a cat family, too, the kitten didn't feel kinship or safe. The visitor was black and huge and powerful. It nudged the cat-carry and then swatted it, once, twice, sending it roughly and rapidly over the edge of the porch and upside down on the earth. The kitten scratched frantically against whatever was next to him and crawled through the tiniest triangle of space. He was now behind a trellis used to seal off the underside of the porch. Vicious eyes peered at him and the black thing hissed and slapped. Then came the man's voice, loud, and quick steps and more yelling, and then the woman's voice. The kitten scrambled farther back to the darkest part under the house, wide-eyed. Terrified.

The next afternoon, when the kitten hadn't appeared and the woman hadn't heard even one mewl, she dressed in work jeans and old, long-sleeved, blue shirt. She took a hammer and hooked the claw of it over the top of a lattice board and worked the lattice loose. She removed one panel and crawled gingerly under the porch. She had a stick in one hand and used that to scrape the ground ahead of her. She was frightened, too, of spiders and snakes.

"Here, kitty," she called, "here kitty." She made clucking sounds, softer clucks than she would have used to call chickens. She made kissing sounds, too, with her lips, because she had often made that sound around the kittens. She wondered why the momma cat had disappeared and now worried that she wouldn't see the white kitten again either. She wanted very much not to be allergic to cats. That kitten's all right, she thought. And so's the momma. Things work out okay.

She crawled back to the front, replaced the lattice but left the nails a little loose. Twice more that day and then three times the next and once the next, she went under the porch and looked into the dark depths. *Come on honey. Come on.*

Momma cat was shut in a rickety cupboard in the barn, where old-fashioned tools were stored. She had followed a flicker of mouse tail, the mouse disappearing under the cupboard, she inside the bottom portion. The man had come through, finishing up his workday, and shut the cupboard. When he opened it two days later, the momma cat meowed harshly in reprimand and then softened, hurrying toward the house and her remaining kitten.

He was gone.

Many creatures were aware of the drama at the human house and the surrounding area—a panther had come slinking in, disturbing everything, even the air, and dogs in neighboring farms had howled and barked. Birds and squirrels and a groundhog with her babies and a raccoon and a possum knew about the kitten. A snake had seen the heat of him and had felt his presence. The kitten was far from the house now, having come out on the north side and in the moonlight headed like a white ghost toward the garden shadows and shelter. He had traveled the rows, aware of that black thing that had wanted him, aware of the woman's voice which was near the black thing. He was searching for her in this new direction, making long forays forward, then resting, blue eyes startled from the unknown. He drank from a little pocket of water in the garden and, at the garden's farthest edge, looked out on an expanse of green so huge to his little world as an ocean would be to a human.

He was hungry. He nibbled on first one thing and then another, not one of them edible. The sun came fully up and he was so frightened at the greatness of it all without one being he recognized that he scurried like a tiny cloud toward the many trees in the distance. He did reach them and in that darkness he hunkered down, let his eyes close a moment, then another moment, then for a while. He dreamed. He woke hungry and went searching in the damp leaves and moist soil and bushes and twigs for nourishment. No one had taught him hunting.

The kitten managed to eat enough to stay alive. A turtle dropped a piece of tadpole, probably by accident, and a bit of insect fell from the pointed, fierce beak of a blue jay. Scraps of scavenged food appeared here and there on the earth. A mother fox considered the white kitten as a possible meal—she, after all, was nursing a set of babies, too, in her den— but she didn't attack this little white one. She felt almost motherly toward him, and so left him unharmed and went looking for the next meal for herself and her kits.

So many different appetites and ways of sharing, and not one doubt that they should or should not eat what they desired and what was available. They were animals and simply what they were. Still, that was a struggling baby there, that white creature, no threat yet. If the panther had come along, the kitten would

14

have no longer had a life. But the panther didn't come.

A big dog, a redbone hound, bounded into the woods and stopped short. His owners were out on the grassy area, which would one day be a dog park, and they had let him off the leash. He was huge and needed to stretch and leap and dash and retrieve. He stopped short, though, floppy ears swaying, droopy eyes fixed on the white kitten. And the kitten, desperate perhaps for some companionship, came up and stroked the dog's forelegs by walking near and weaving around them, meowing plaintively. The dog looked over his shoulder quickly, then back down at the kitten. He nudged it with his nose, quickly but gently. Did so again. It leaned more forcefully against him, purred. The hound barked upward, meaning it for his owners, but the kitten scurried. The hound barked, which in his language meant "come back don't worry," but the kitten backed off a little more and hissed. Hissed. The redbone knew cats and hisses but he also knew this was a kitten. No danger. He stopped barking. He wagged his tail, dangled his tongue, and tossed his head. In a few seconds, the kitten returned, but by then the dog's humans were calling. He turned away, bounded out onto the grass and told his owners about the kitten in so many barks. They came close to the woody area but peered cautiously and didn't advance. "I wonder what he sees?"

"Maybe we don't want to know," her partner said, and in a few minutes they walked away, calling the hound after them. The kitten moved toward the open space, meowed, but held back. A hawk or something was soaring, and the shadow swept over the field and the retreating beings.

The Finding of Zeno

In September, when the leaves of Cave Hollow Park were a thick explosion of amber and rust and yellow and red, and dark green, and pale green, and patches of all of them lay in big and little spots, and leaves fluttered over the field and sailed and wafted in the air, the white kitten was very frail. Very thin. His small face was so bony that he was almost a skeleton already. Why could he not fend for himself? Hunt? Though the creatures around him didn't have those words, they had that awareness— of a brave animal, yet timid. He was a cat but not quite. A baby being. The birds didn't dart at him, though they watched him. He walked the same path, one that he had first taken. He was the path cat then. His tiny tail was erect when he walked, a bold sign, giving him away. In the darker undergrowth and at night, it was like a flag on a tiny ship sailing through their land.

But he was going to die. Such a likelihood announced itself even without words.

Perhaps the kitten knew it. On a warm and windy afternoon, Josh Becker came to Cave Hollow Park just to enjoy the sweep of fall day. Usually he had his two dogs with him, but not today. He had been in his workshop most of the day and was on the way home. He was about twenty, very thin, with black hair and green eyes, pale green. They might have been hazel at times, but usually they were more definitely green. He was standing stock still in the middle of the flat expanse, the grass now browning and dry. He had his arms out and his head back, having just inhaled deeply.

Something ran up his body, truly ran, over foot, up left leg, over stomach, and was climbing to his chest, stopping over his heart. It happened so quickly that he saw what it was just as he realized what had happened.

A small white cat—a kitten, really—clung to him. It meowed a bit harshly, again, almost a human cry.

Rabid? he thought, but only briefly and not seriously. He knew. Hungry. It was so terribly thin.

"And who are you?" he said, cupping the tiny skull in his left palm while he slid his right hand

18

under the kitten's behind and carefully lifted him up and away from his chest. The claws clung then released, and he held the kitten again close, crooking his elbow for its perch. "It's okay. I got you." He strode toward his car, murmuring the whole time. It wasn't a purr, but the sound might have been similar to the kitten, who again climbed up Josh when Josh was driving, all the way to his shoulder and tried to get on his head but didn't. It meowed, too. "I know," Josh said. "I'm getting us home as fast as I can. You're going to be all right."

At a traffic light, he called home and asked his wife to shut Speeds and Lucky in the garage. "A kitten just asked me for help," he said. "It's the darndest thing. It might as well be talking."

When Josh's wife saw the kitten, now lowered to the linoleum-covered floor, her heart wrenched. "It's starving," she said. "Who would have left it out there?"

"Maybe it got lost. Don't think about it."

She opened a fresh can of evaporated milk, poured only a tiny amount in the saucer. "I think we can't feed him too much so fast. Isn't that right? It could make him sick?"

The kitten lapped up the cream and continued licking the saucer until the wife,

Wilma, took it away. She added a thin layer of cream and pinched into it pieces of white bread. She put it in the floor.

"Even starving, there's a grace to how he eats," she said.

They fashioned a safe place for the kitten in the laundry room, a box filled with rags, a dish of water, and covered the floor with newspapers.

Josh went to the store after kitty food and kitty litter and proper dishes for a small creature.

Wilma had shut the door to the laundry room and the kitten cried. She wouldn't open the door right then, but when the kitten fell silent, she opened it and allowed the little thing to come out. The kitten stretched, the sweetest, most comfortable kind of stretch, first one paw out and then the other, head and forebody dipping low, as if just waking and limbering the body ready to start the day.

She thought that from his features, "Skull" might be a good name. But then, he was beautiful in some ways, like a sculpture, and she wanted a better name.

"Zeno," Josh suggested, having come home.

"Ugh."

"I like the sound of it, and it's the last letter

of the alphabet. You know. He made it just in time."

"Who was Zeno?"

"A philosopher. He wasn't a great one. He argued there couldn't be both many things and not many things."

"Which means?"

"It's a paradox."

"Zeno," Wilma murmured, looking at the newest member of their household. "It's a soft sound. And sort of majestic."

Out at Cave Hollow Park a kind of whisper went around, not words, not even thoughts, but like a feeling, an awareness that every creature shared, just as they shared the air and the sunlight and the darkness and the need to sleep.

The kitten was no longer in their midst. The kitten was not of this territory anymore. But it had been there. It was part of the history of their world. A white kitten, fearful, but still with firm ways, endurance. Its tail was always erect when it walked, like a standard it bore.

The Neighborhood

Zeno slept in short spans, without truly lying down. He hunched. Gradually, as he fell into sleep, his body did relax. Surely he had cat dreams, about his early family and the warmth of that time, like a blanket he could cover with when he wasn't wakeful and having to worry about food and safety, and without following his natural curiosity and longing to play, common to all cats, especially little ones, and possibly to all creatures. Maybe even plants are blessed with curiosity. The laundry room was safe, yes, but confining. No soil, no rich scent of must and life, plant and animal, fur and skin and blossom and bark and bird and nest. There were smells here, too, and sounds.

Dogs. Two of them. One small and intense, control smoldering from her perfectly neat, compact body. She was a husky type but contained. The other, twice her size, was male, tense but fluid, ready, assessing the cat, but acknowledging no danger and feigning no interest. Both dogs understood that the mistress, their beloved female human, wanted to hold the cat, and wished no harm to it. She made soft sounds which they knew named the cat for them and said "Good dogs. Good boy. Good girl." They understood. The little cat was "Zeno," said with a rise and fall like mothers to babies.

Zeno, in Wilma's lap, smelled the long-time presence of dogs, their intensity and their power. He didn't look in their direction at first, but stoically stared straight ahead. The stroking of his back was comforting but also restricting. If he moved even slightly, the hand held him. Through the screen door came the scents of fall outside and strange scents, too, a hot one associated with a rushing sound that increased, slowed, came again. Clattering. He heard a confusing blend of jangle and whisper, natural and unnatural sounds. He had left woods and had run to a human and now he was in a world his ears and nose couldn't identify.

Zeno looked sideways, directly at the largest dog, who gently but quickly sniffed Zeno, very close, then backed away, studied him a few seconds more, and walked over to the door. Zeno watched, expecting in his cat knowledge that the dog could perhaps open the door. But he couldn't. He only looked.

Zeno turned his attention to the smaller dog. And knew, from scent and from the feelings the dog revealed in eyes and quivering body and quivering sensibilities throughout, that this little dog was female. Zeno felt warmth toward her. He stayed where he was, delicately touched and held by Wilma. When he sensed she was about to stand, Zeno leapt easily down to the yellow linoleum floor. The big dog noticed and turned away from the door, alert and watching. The smaller dog was fascinated. Her eyes would have been round with excitement but they couldn't take that shape. Zeno knew. She knew. Wilma, too, knew, but held silent and still. This was an important moment. It was Zeno's moment.

Zeno, on four feet, tail erect, up like a flag, walked purposefully and easily toward the small dog, toward Speeds. Zeno slid his white body against Speed's right leg, across the narrow chest, against the left leg, began purring, and turned, leaning even closer to the dark-furred female, purring deeply, turned again, and again. Speeds looked shocked, up at Wilma and then partly down, just rolling her eyes and barely dipping her head. She was enduring the attention. It wasn't an assault and yet it was so strange to her. She was a dog, being stroked by a cat, wooed by a cat. Her warm heart, always loyal to Wilma and to Josh, and even to Lucky, the border collie, beat faster and warmer, and a flush of fondness forever filled her. Zeno. This cat was her cat.

Though Wilma wanted to get her camera or phone and take a snapshot of Zeno and Speeds, she didn't want to leave the three creatures alone. Not yet. She scooped Zeno up. "You brave sweet thing." She put him in the laundry room, closed the door. "Good dogs," she said, and opened the screen door for them. She followed them out on the deck and opened the gate to the stairway down to the yard. She closed the gate. This would be a good set-up for the three. When Zeno wanted to be away from the dogs, he could always rest on the deck. If he wanted down, when it was safe, he could jump to the railing and walk down the stair railing. He could duck under the railing, too. The ground was only five feet away at the highest—not too much for a cat. He might be too small now. She wasn't sure, having never lived with a cat before.

Zeno recognized the cat-carry. He knew it wasn't the same one as before, but it was the same kind of structure. Safe and not safe. He hunkered inside, head lowered and eyes down. He meowed his distress three times, adding a hollow sound that only now came to him, something he was capable of that felt right at this moment. It meant *out*, and *misery*, and *help*, and *stop*. He went quiet. Wilma was taking him to the veterinarian, but what Zeno knew was motion that he wasn't making. Motion of the world beneath and around him, and strange sounds. He waited. He saw outside again, was swung this way and that, heard a voice, "Sorry, Zeno. Sorry." Then the world stopped moving. He smelled many creatures other than humans and saw strange objects outside the cat-carry, so he was grateful for its safety. He made one extended hollow meow protest. Then silent again.

He was lifted out, stood on something cold and bright, too bright. Three humans were around him and Wilma, his human, was farther away. He heard the sound they used with him most, "Zeno," "Good boy, Zeno," and now other sounds: "That's it." "This won't hurt." "Just a minute now." "Okay." "You're doing good." All of this was slightly familiar, but the accompanying touches were too strange and unpleasant. When the cat-carry was placed next to him and the door opened, he slipped into it and went to the very back of it, turning around and facing the front, calmed when the tiny gate closed. They could see him but he was truly inside. Separate. He hunkered and waited.

Wilma's voice was soft, like a purr. Again the swinging and the sunny world, so pleasant. The moving vehicle and harsh sounds, but still sun, and air, and scents. He meowed, not a protest. He came to the front of the cat-carry, put one paw against it. Meowed.

"In a minute, baby. We're almost home."

Wilma set the cat-carry on the back deck, put a little water and dry cat food inside it. "You can get used to this, huh? You're safe."

The smells here were already a little familiar. This was the house of the two dogs. And his house. He pushed against the grate door, pressed his nose against it. He could see most of the porch. He saw something worrying a few feet away, black, heard it panting slightly. He smelled her. The dog that liked him.

28

He meowed a different sound. It was a communication, meant something like "Hello. I'm here. I'm okay."

Early morning, late September, with the little crackly whispers of leaves and the sweet melody of breezes, whistles and rustles, bird songs, and bird warnings, plans for flight, rustle of wings, the perfume of dried berries and dried petals, fresh seed under strewn straw, caught moisture under a blanket of remaining grass. Nearby, the rushing of cars and bicycles, voices of students walking to class. From the southeast, a high barking—a small dog, chained probably. From the direct east, a deep, powerful bark, three in succession, almost rumbling the earth.

Zeno was lowered carefully by Wilma onto the deck railing. A huge tree just a few feet away arced over the deck, still with a few leaves clinging. Zeno could leap to the tree or to the ground or walk the railing to the left or right and at a corner to the north. But he sat where he was placed. He sat very regally for a small cat, front paws before and slightly between back paws, front legs straight, head high but not rigid. His green eyes seemed placid, but his mind was absorbing the landscape nearest him and that farther away. It wasn't as huge a world as the one he had entered from the woods, not a flat plain of emptiness bordered on two sides by trees. This one had the dwelling behind him, very broad and tall, safe. Rows of trees on each side and other trees grouped farther down on one side. On the other, the trees stopped, and the tops of something appeared. Houses, and university grounds, though Zeno couldn't know that. Houses he was coming to understand, and cars. Some words he understood, though he didn't indicate so. He couldn't and wouldn't if he could. To look stoic was natural, though the degree to which he could do it was one of his individual gifts. His searching eyes took in many hiding places, shadowy clusters of dead leaves or stalks, wide trunks, clumps of soil by a tree, a pile of rocks, something huge and dark with many flies swarming and the smell of decaying food. He stretched, yawned, walked to one corner of the railing, sat again. In about half an hour, he leapt down from the railing, and squeezed between the metal posts of the gate to the front yard.

Inside the house, Wilma panicked and went out quietly on the deck to peer around the house corner and see where Zeno was—

headed for the front. She dashed inside and through the kitchen, dining room, and living room to the front door. She opened it but didn't go outside. He should feel free but protected and watched. When his white form appeared, walking leisurely, tail slightly waving from side to side, she opened the screen door just enough to let her voice be clear. "Stay in the yard, Zeno. Stay." She didn't think he would understand but she would reinforce that word now and then and call "No!" if he started into the street.

He came to the walk leading from the front sidewalk to the small porch. He sat in the middle of that private walkway. On either side of him vines still green looped up and over and fell partly on the concrete steps. A redbud tree and plum tree shared the yard to his right, and to his left, back where he had just walked, were two pear trees. His private land. His little trees. He heard a familiar bark. Speeds. Across the street, from a building much longer than his building, came a stream of children, loud and fast, and he startled so much that he could have run for cover or run accidentally before the coming cars, or up one of the trees. But he stayed still as if he weren't afraid. A few school children noticed him and one small girl waved. Zeno, though he looked calm and brave, was thinking of where he had once been, with others like him, sleeping and crawling over one another. It was warm and he was full and content. He waited long enough that the little squirrel who owned the neighbor's tall fir tree and often visited the school grounds saw him. The squirrel studied the size of the cat and assessed his nature. He was thin, the cat, but that didn't mean he wasn't strong. He was just thin and quiet. A little bigger than a squirrel.

"He doesn't eat much," Wilma told Josh. "I offered him tuna today. He just wants the dry and a bit of cream."

"He seems bored with food, doesn't he?"

"Maybe. Maybe he was too hungry for so long that he doesn't recognize hunger much."

"Wouldn't it work the other way?" Josh was ladling tuna gravy over toast. "If he's been starved, he should wolf down food, take all he can get."

"Not Zeno."

"Maybe there's a special food he wants," Wilma said, knowing that was true.

"Like what?"

"Maybe it's not what, but where. He would eat more in some company. His family."

"I bet you're right," Josh said.

When they cleaned the kitchen, Josh put a scant teaspoon of tuna gravy into Zeno's clean dish and put it out on the railing next to Zeno. "How's this, fellow?"

Zeno smelled it, turned and lapped at it twice. Then he leapt down from the railing and asked in at the door. He sallied in, looking for Speeds. She was sleeping on the sofa, where she wasn't allowed. He jumped up next to her and stretched alongside. He cleaned his front paws while Speeds raised her head up, puzzled, looking around the room for the answer to why this cat did this and how was she supposed to feel about it and what was she to do. Part of her ached to comfort the smaller creature; part of her thought it was too late, or too something— beyond her.

Zeno could run. He sped across the fall yard, past the two staring dog residents, and zipped up the chinaberry tree, zipped way up the tallest part of the trunk, hung there a minute without looking at any of them. The sky was spatters of blue through the branches, and spatters of white, and when the few leaves and twigs shivered the sky shivered and he felt frightened and powerful at the same time. He went backward quickly, too, and leapt free of the tree with only a couple feet to go. He sped past the dogs, around the yard, and up the tree by the deck, stopped at the first thick side branch. His white slender arms were splayed out, the back ones too, like a white flying squirrel. He pulled up a foot, turned in a dizzying quickness and leapt to the railing of the deck. His heart beat fast and he felt a swelling in his chest, just a good feeling to him, a perfect feeling from what he had done. Run. Run.

When he ran through the house in such a way, Wilma called it "thunderrunning."

"He's showing off," she said. "He wants us to admire him and to approve of him."

Josh agreed. When he went outside and Zeno was there, Zeno always displayed some feat, usually a wild frantic rush up a tree and then down and sometimes immediately up again.

He was unbelievably quick.

"I wish," Josh said, "he could demonstrate that to whatever it was meant to be demonstrated to."

"Maybe other cats?"

"Maybe an enemy."

"Oh! Let's hope he doesn't have any." Wilma shuddered at the idea of any threat to any of her creatures.

It must be said that Zeno had the traits of a good birder, which meant he would soon be able to catch birds. All the feathered creatures in the back yard and the nearby yards had already spotted him. Thus far, he stayed in his own territory and only grew skilled at movements. They didn't know of his history during the starving period, what he had eaten, how it had been given him. But his muscles knew, and his eyes, and his hearing, and his nose. He knew that he was quick, quick, quick, and could leap and hook, and catch. And bite. But. He didn't do it yet. Something would overtake him one day, something natural and driving. He didn't think about or anticipate it in any way except that his body attended closely the small creatures who were often in his path. He was a cat. Cats hunt mice and birds, and lizards, and other little things. Not from choice. They were made so.

Some things were by choice. Zeno was a gentle cat.

A not gentle cat often came up the alley from a corner house where he and five other cats were well fed by an older woman. She was bent almost double and used a cane but she fed creatures regularly. If one was sick, she would try to lure it into a cat-carry and take it to the veterinarian. She paid the medical bills. She kept a rickety old shed filled with straw and rags so neighborhood cats could sleep out of the weather. She didn't let them in her house. Actually, more than five used her property, but only the five would allow her near them.

The one who strolled up the alley was male, like Zeno, and solid gray. Short-haired gray, with amberish eyes and a straight, broad nose. He looked like a bully cat, which, unfortunately, he was. He liked to fight. And he had ways of showing his prowess, just how vicious he could be. He would drop to his side and move his rear legs as if he were slashing something to pieces with them. Slashing. He would do that in front of another cat. If cats grin, and some certainly seem to, he grinned. The old woman had named him Arthur.

Zeno slipped between the gate posts at the end of the back yard. The dogs were at attention on the inside, watching him with mouths open. They seemed envious or a little agitated. It must have seemed unfair to watch another creature who shared the same house and family simply leave with total freedom, squeeze through a gate. Both canines neared the exit spot, and Speeds pressed her nose toward the bottom gap. The gate didn't give. She had gained only a dusty muzzle, and she was an exceedingly neat dog. She rubbed her nose against the top of her paw. Lucky looked at the fence. It wasn't that high and he could jump it at any time. There were little triangles of wire, though, that could catch on hair or skin. That had happened once. Besides, he was a border collie, very obedient by nature, and he had been instructed never to jump the fence again. Never. He knew the sound and that it meant No. He didn't likely understand the length of time intended by the word.

Zeno walked a few yards to his left, tail high, then turned right, staying at the edge of that narrow road, with houses on the both sides, until he reached the big road. There, he stopped and after watching many huge, noisy vehicles pass, he turned right, by the sidewalk but actually at the edge of the road. At the main road, which was very broad, cars roared, wind gusted, and wheels whined. He got on the rise, which was a curb, with dead grass for about a foot inward. He walked along that traffic lane, at the same steady pace, with his tail swaying a little, and

the tip of the tail curling forward only a least
bit. It was almost a jaunty look. Confident. He
didn't feel confident. He felt he had to walk
in that way and had to keep his tail straight. It
was something about owning a place to be or
being able to walk within that space. He had
done that in the long-ago woods, maybe not
long ago. Cats have no sense of true linear
time. But it seemed long ago because he didn't
have that place anymore. He didn't want to
be hungry. Had he been really hungry? Yes. Yes.
He remembered and was terribly sad for a few
seconds. He didn't sit down. He commenced
walking again, turning right and continuing until
he was passing his own place, where the four
trees marked two sides of the yard. He turned
to his right, which was south, then alongside the
house and fence. Speeds and Lucky, both lying
down, watched him end up his daily trek. He
was coming again toward the gate itself which
he would enter his way, by squeezing between
the posts at the bottom, when he was stopped
by a sudden movement and a sound. The dogs
heard the sound. Not cat hiss. Not bark. A kind of
low, wet snarl, from the back of a throat through
a wide-open mouth.

Mean cat.

Zeno stood where he was, tail still erect. After a few seconds, he sat down in his normal fashion, regally, and seemed totally unafraid. He hadn't seen a fight, hadn't yet fought. He had many lovely moves, some of them fierce, but he hadn't played long with brothers or sisters. Hadn't played much. The other cat, Arthur to humans, suddenly yawned and lay down. He looked away, toward the cement parking lot beyond. Zeno looked leisurely toward the gate, back at the rear of Arthur's head, and at the gate. He walked toward it in his normal pace but he didn't feel normal. And he shouldn't have. In a split second Arthur was up and had slammed both front paws down at the base of Zeno's tail, down with claws out, puncturing. Zeno was driven by shock and pain to run up the wire of the fence and his claws caught so Arthur was able to slam his leg. Zeno dragged himself to the top wire-triangles and fell over the other side, catching one arm in a triangle. All the while Speeds was yelping her heart out and snapping at the fence and at Arthur. Lucky was silently running like a wolf along the back edge, fierce, ready to get through if a way came. Wilma's voice cut through the air and Arthur like a shot was streaking down the alley, just a short distance. Then he stopped and watched the back yard, looking for the white cat. That new cat. That scrawny one that boxed off the yard with that stupid walk, high-tail walk.

Zeno had broken his right forearm. He was in pain but was also perplexed. What had caused that? What was he to have done? Was there no place for him? This was his place.

Wilma stroked his head. She cried, too. She put him on a blanket and very gently carried him outside to the car. She called Josh, who was about to leave his shop anyway. He met her at the veterinarian's office.

In the back yard, the atmosphere was tense. Speeds paced for a while, and made a few yelping sounds, more to herself than to any creature. Lucky lay down in the corner beyond the gate as if sleeping. His ears were on duty.

The birds twittered and winged from one tree to another for a while, avoiding the open housetops and gutters. They chirped and probably passed on the story. The old woman down the alley fed birds, too. So many of the humans did. And dogs were everywhere, some fenced in, some tied or chained, some out only for walks. The people in this house, where the white cat lived, sometimes carried toads out of their yard and put them in the neighbors' thick bushes. They put suet out in the winter, front and back. Corn for the squirrels. Water here and there. Toad houses.

Now they had attracted that gray cat.

Zeno had a white cast on his forearm. His paw was partway free from it and he could move his shoulder and elbow. The first night with it he hunkered and waited. He was in the upstairs bedroom in a soft, round, cat bed. A little box was right next to it. He could smell the presence of his humans and the warmth of the house. Speeds was in the room, sleeping on a rug, her nose toward Zeno. Lucky was downstairs, in a dog bed under a long table desk. Zeno didn't really sleep, but he dozed. He was partly drugged and his body felt like it wasn't his own. He had felt that way before. He waited for it to pass or for whatever happened next. He did bow his head a little and closed his eyes. He would have welcomed the comfort of a cat who loved him, a mother or sibling, or just a friendly cat who communicated without words. He hunkered even lower, remembered a big gray cat. He didn't have words but he had the concepts and the experience. Hurt. Fear. He understood that he would squeeze through the gate again. He didn't have any choice. He was the white cat who walked a path. That's what he had done. He had stayed alive doing that and that's what he knew to do.

So. When he could walk again, the gray cat might be there. What would he do?

Adapting to Injury

Always now, lurking in Zeno's mind, was the image of the gray cat, Arthur, and the feeling of the entire attack incident. Zeno could remember parts of it vividly, the sight of the gray Arthur, the sound of the snarl, the tug of his own claws against wire, the dig of the other's claws. The shame, or whatever it is a cat feels that is their concept of shame. A knowledge that some cat might have faced the gray down, might have swatted that haughty face, might have made him cower, slink away. Zeno, thinking of this one day on the deck, safe in the sun, eyeing the alley and knowing that in that shadow was Arthur the Gray, sat up, then stood, and stretched upward, sort of twisted his body thinner and taller and arched his neck and showed his teeth and walked backward. To a cardinal watching from a cable line to the house, Zeno seemed to have become a different cat. The cardinal was fascinated. He arched his own neck, and spread his wings as if to let the breeze sail beneath them. Then he fluttered them still. Zeno had unspiraled himself and was the white cat again, placid and quiet. Then Zeno did it again suddenly, and the cardinal shot red and straight to one of the three plum trees along the back fence. His brown mate was there. He was beside her, unsettled still, little hints of threat, threat, threat. They calmed down together. Zeno was on the railing, even with the white cast on his forearm. He preened, moistening his upper legs and chest and appearing to glance only casually at the yard, his gaze sliding past the rear gate.

Zeno saw mostly the gate, though he didn't look at it. He wanted to be squeezing between the post now and on his trek. His legs wanted to walk, wanted to pace regularly and steadily. His paws wanted to feel the change from dry grass to pebbly soil, to asphalt, to cement, to curb grass. He wanted to travel center-way between the tiny yapping corner dog and the huge, gruff woofing giant dog on the east. Those two couldn't reach him and they bore him no ill will. They were part of the music of his walk, part of the pace.

But the cast. It wasn't heavy, but it wasn't

arm. Not *arm.* With his pink tongue he cleaned between the pads of his feet, and around the claws. The paws couldn't walk, so to ease his longing he washed them thusly for a long time.

Josh came out on the deck and crumpled something on the railing beside Zeno.

"Wilma thinks you might like this."

Zeno could sense the warmth of it. He liked that, and the smell, but he couldn't show his interest yet. He had to wait and glance at it and then look away, toward the fence. Even ignoring the new substance, he was very drawn to it. He wanted Josh to move away. Zeno stood up on all fours and retreated from the warm bits, looking now at Josh and purring just a little.

Josh responded, stroking Zeno, who pushed his back up round into Josh's palm, over and over. With his thumb, Josh rubbed the spot between Zeno's ears, and in a minute or so switched to rubbing under Zeno's chin with a forefinger. Zeno withdrew.

"Okay." Josh understood. The petting was welcome and nice, but it was over now. "You going to eat this chicken?" He tapped the railing next to the food.

Zeno looked at it and then at Josh.

Josh studied the calm, pretty face. "You're

still skinny, you know. You could put some weight on. It's chicken. Wilma will feel better if you eat it." Josh emphasized the last two words, but in a kind way, raising his eyebrows as if he and Zeno, both males, understood what the female Wilma was like. Josh tapped the railing again. "Chicken."

Now Zeno could approach the good-smelling gift. He sat close to it, hunkered down casually, and nibbled at one piece. He ate it slowly. Then nibbled at another. He sat up, looked at the alley.

Josh tapped the railing. "Don't worry about that cat. Chicken." Tap. Tap. "Chicken."

Zeno returned to nibbling, slowly and delicately, until just small traces remained, traces that a truly hungry cat, an eating cat, might make disappear, might lick away.

"Good boy." Josh rubbed the between-ears spot fondly and firmly. "Wilma!" He turned toward the house. "You were right."

Zeno surveyed the back yard and alley and gradually a bit of fear rose in him. He was familiar with fear and with alertness, more familiar than with total ease. Now the tension was smoothed somewhat by the taste of that food. He had eaten more than usual at one time, more than he wanted. It was the man's presence and his strong desire which Zeno had felt and responded to as best he could.

With the cast on, Zeno could leap to the washer or the dryer. He could leap to the sofa, walk along the sofa back, thunderrun up the stairs and down, bound onto the bed, run ducked low from one kitchen chair seat to the other, full circle around, swatting at Lucky or Speeds even if they were out of reach, displaying such grace and speed and agility. The dogs were appreciative of that, though they hadn't seen a cat up close in intimate surroundings like this before. They realized this was a truly admirable creature. They were stronger than it was, the white cat, but it could out-maneuver them. Maybe even better than a squirrel. They didn't know much about squirrels except the aggravating habit squirrels had of circling a tree trunk just out of reach of the dog's mouth, round and round, shifting right, left, in the blink of an eye.

Zeno, though, was theirs, and magnificent.

Zeno ran up tree trunks with the cast, higher and higher, and when he did, he looked for the gray.

The cast was frayed and dirty. Zeno was at

the gate. A few bricks were half buried under the swinging part. Josh and Wilma had wanted the dogs not to be able to dig out. But between the swinging part and the post there was only soil. Zeno dug at it. Without too much effort his head went through. He pressed belly down flatter, thrust backward with his hind legs, and he was on the other side of the gate, safe, sitting, looking calmly around, but heart beating fast. He turned to his left, tail coming up, flag high, as he took the first lap of his missing daily walk. Oh, his legs felt good, his back, his lungs. This was Zeno's life. He was near happy. But in his mind, ready he was for an ugliness to leap on him.

It was there, too, that ugliness. Arthur the Gray lay under a car in the neighbor's yard, watching the white cat return to the territory, marching again. Arthur lay very still, head up, eyes narrowed and intent. He did enjoy power and threat and the hunt for power. He was big and had been successful at being the main cat. He was willing to get hurt, to take a scratch or a jab. He would just jab back harder. And he had learned how to come up from behind, to bite and claw at the retreating cat. What could one do? Even if it turned to strike, Arthur was able to hit and stay and hit again. His body was a tough one.

Now his keen eyes knew where to look to catch a glimpse of the white tail here and there, around the block. When he sensed that the cat was nearing the front of the house and would be coming back down the length of the back fence, Arthur crawled out and yawned and stretched. It was October, cool, but with a bright sun flickering through bare branches, and for a few moments the shadows over the cement made him stare and remember something of his own history. He was a daydreaming cat at that moment, and didn't see, didn't think of, there being another cat nearby.

Zeno came around the east rear fence corner feeling he must run to the gate and scramble under it quickly, before anything gray could jump him. He didn't hurry though. He turned gracefully, saw Arthur lying just beyond the gate, down flat, on his side, stretched almost out of sight. Arthur raised his head, came up to a sitting position, paws together, eyes slitted but aimed in Zeno's direction. Zeno was still standing, looking at the little entrance he had to his own yard, and to the cat just inches past it. He had to do it. He had to go forward and try to get in. He glanced up at the fence top and back at

Arthur. Zeno's desire was clear though he didn't seem hurried or frightened. He longed to leap up and away. He looked at the depression that he had dug for himself. He dropped his gaze to his own paw, lifted it, and cleaned it with his tongue.

Speeds and Lucky had both come out the garage doggy door. Speeds yelped high, and Arthur did look that way, only briefly, then back at Zeno. Lucky crept low, totally in sight, but in work mode, to the fence behind Arthur. Arthur saw the fence had not disappeared, so he was safe from the biggest dog. He returned his hostile look to Zeno.

Speeds yipped every few seconds. Lucky lay as if he could spring forward and through the wire upon command. Zeno and Arthur held their positions. No one appeared from the house, not Josh, not Wilma. No human came up the alley. And even if they had, even if Zeno had taken a momentary distraction to slip into the depression, he couldn't have pulled his backside through. No distraction that wasn't immediately close and threatening would stop Arthur. Arthur's body felt ready for what he had trained himself to do—to hurt timid cats, to gain all the food and all the territory.

50

Zeno was going to go for the entrance to his yard. He was going to do it. But not this moment. Almost. He took two steps that direction and saw the glint in Arthur's eyes. Zeno stopped.

From the alley, from under a hyacinth bush along Wilma and Josh's back fence, came another cat. He just came out, as if he had been sleeping there and only now awakened, which may have been the case. Cats do that. He was a big cat, but not fat, tall and muscular. He was gray and white, with strikingly balanced markings, so he looked to be wearing a gray vest and gray hat and have a gray-tipped tail. His throat and belly were white; his rump and legs were gray on the back, white on the front; his paws were white. He looked almost as if he were wearing a suit. He was a handsome, strange cat, with a very broad nose. He walked leisurely up from the alley, making straight for Arthur. When he was just a foot away from the mean gray cat, the new one lay down, fully, on his side. He stretched in that prone position, so his arm naturally elongated toward Arthur but against the ground, not an attack. With his head arched back, his face was visible to Zeno and Zeno's face to him. They saw one another for a second, and then the new cat let his body relax from the stretch.

People might think that a cat lying down in the presence of another is a submissive action, saying *I'm not threatening, you're the biggest, and I concede that you are master to me. You can hurt me. I concede.* But that isn't always the case. Sometimes the most powerful cat lies down, saying *I'm the biggest. I could make you run, make you leave the territory, make you starve. I am big enough to injure you terribly. To kill you. But I don't want to - I prefer peace and comfort. I like everyone to get along.* This new cat slid his head back again to look at Zeno, that white cat sitting there so beautifully. So sadly. The new cat raised head and shoulders and then smoothly came to a full sitting position. That's all he did. That and look at Zeno.

Zeno understood that he was to enter his yard if he wished to, and he did wish to. Without trembling, though his heart trembled, he walked to the gate and pushed his cast arm and the other one through, head low and through, and tugged the rest of himself along. He walked a few paces into the yard, accompanied by Speeds who smelled him quickly, dividing her attention to the new cat also. Lucky had stood up. The new cat didn't attempt to follow Zeno's route. He walked the outside fence to where it joined the house. There a post was next to the shingles. No fence, no triangles. The gap was far too narrow for any cat, but he jumped onto the ball of the post, his front paws going over and easing his slide down. Practiced, perhaps. Maybe he had visited this house before.

Zeno was now on the deck railing. Lucky and Speeds accompanied the new cat who walked very slowly, allowing their sniffs and sudden stiffness, as if they weren't at all sure if he was allowed in this yard. He made it gradually to the deck stairs, up them, curving around the post, between two slats and onto the deck. Then he jumped up on the railing, sitting in the same pose as Zeno, but not with such beauty. Zeno had the more delicate shape, the patience and grace of his heritage and of his experiences. He was resting. He was glad of this new cat, but he didn't know yet what it meant. Was the new one mean in a different way? Was this no longer Zeno's territory? Zeno knew he hadn't been hurt. But the gray Arthur was still out there. The world was more populated than before. Zeno wasn't sure of his place. He cleaned his paws.

When Wilma came home, she looked out the kitchen door and saw two cats lying on the railing, facing one another. She was alarmed in a way, because it could be a stalemate, a fight about to begin. They looked almost drowsy, but who knew with cats? She moved to the window by the stove, so she could see the length of yard. Nothing untoward. She opened the door to the garage, and the two dogs blundered in, neither jumping on her, but both simply being too close and too ready to please.

"I guess everything's all right," she said, "since you guys aren't acting up."

She checked on the cats again, cautiously, not touching the door, only looking through the window. "Well."

She fed Speeds and Lucky, both of whom had little bits of chicken added to their dry food. Then she got Zeno's dish and an old saucer. She put shreds of chicken and some dry food onto each saucer, held them on one hand and wrist, and opened the back door. Both cats sat up and looked at her. She pushed the screen door out, speaking as she did. "What have we here, Zeno? Company?" The new cat did tense up. Wilma suspected he would jump to the ground, so she stood where she was. "I have food here, Zeno. Zeno. Do you want it?" She took a step toward the railing and the new cat was gone, down, running into the middle of the yard, stopping. Sitting.

"Hello kitty," she called in a soft tone, looking out at the new one, but moving slowly toward Zeno. "Hello kitty," broken into syllables, softly and rhythmically. "Hello kitty."

She put both saucers on the railing, one immediately before Zeno, and the other about two feet away, to her left. She went inside and over to the window above the stove. She saw the new one move toward the house, out of her sight. She hurried back to the door window. There he or she was. Probably a he because of the sheer size of him. A very handsome fellow. He looked at the door. Smart guy too. She had appeared from there, so he suspected that's where she was. She didn't touch the door or open it.

Let them have their dinner, she thought, then said it to herself and to the dogs, like a pleasant gift. "Let them have their dinner. Let the cats have their dinner in peace. You had yours."

"I was so glad to see it," she told Josh. "I think we have to keep the new one if we can. He's outside. It won't hurt us."

Josh wasn't sure. "It may mean vet bills. It's

another commitment."

"Let's just see what happens. We don't have to decide tonight."

Josh and Wilma went out the front door and stole down the far outside fence, looking toward their own yard. The dogs were outside, Speeds peering off west, Lucky nosing along the back fence. And there, lying on the railing of the high deck, were two cats. Heads up, front paws dangling over the edge. It felt so good, that moment, the peace and harmony of it. Birds were still awake, but silent. Evening feeding had passed. Neighbors who put out seeds were refilling birdfeeders. Squirrels were running the high wires and leaping branches in the last before-bedtime games and duties. Traffic had slowed. Lights came on. Flickers of television screens filled rooms and reflected on windows. Laughter and music came in slow drifts.

Arthur the Gray had gone back and eaten his fill at the old woman's house. He wouldn't be going into the shed for hours yet. He liked to hunt at night, around trash cans and into some basements, and under houses. He teased the big dog at times.

He thought of the new cat at the white cat's house. He knew that one. The big one. He had been around a long time, and never did anything but just what he had done today. Arthur had a vision of the cat stretching out long and tilting his head to look at the white one. Arthur didn't understand it, but he didn't question it. A team. Two cats now. They liked each other. A different situation. With the thought of the white one, an anger rose up, but it faded. He wasn't a planning creature.

And so, a pleasant time settled over that corner of the block, town, and world. Zeno walked daily, alone, because his companion, his adopted brother, was a mellow cat. He strolled in his own way, down the alley and occasional loops past other interesting places. There was a female gray cat far down the block, and though Wilma and Josh had the new cat neutered, so he would not father children to run wild and perhaps hungry, he still liked the female. He liked all female cats. He would show fondness and affection by not taking their food, not being cruel or dominant. He would gently lick the back of the female's neck, but not for long. It was almost a courtesy of male to female cats to do so. Even males would groom each other as signs of brotherhood. Not all, but some.

Zeno was terribly fond of Tristan, the new

family member, but he didn't demonstrate his feelings. They usually slept in the house at night, but occasionally would stay gone and out of sight, perhaps joining the old woman's group, now that Tristan was a constant safety for Zeno, or perhaps going mousing (shameful idea to us humans but cats are hunters), or just exploring trash cans and cluttered, exotic places. They ate at about 7:00 a.m., when Wilma or Josh gave them food on cat saucers, either in the laundry room, on the dryer where the dogs could not reach the dishes before they were gathered up, or on the deck—if Zeno and Tristan had asked out before eating. They were together on the railing often, Zeno sitting up and Tristan lying down. The house was blue and the deck had been painted the same, but the paint was peeling. It was a charming look from the outside, from all angles, but particularly warmly appealing when viewed from the back, with the dogs in the yard and the two cats on the blue railing. The cats would lie also in their own yard, front and back, and on the sidewalk to the house, and on the little front porch—just a three-steps-up to concrete block, with wrought-iron railing, scroll top, and a bench on either side of the block, green to the left and red to the right. They might lie one to a bench, both on top or both under, or one up and one down. A good pair of buddies.

No grooming, though, and no playing. When Zeno played, it was alone, that wondrous thunderrunning up the chinaberry or the mulberry (not the plum trees, they were too small), then spinning down, alarming and amusing birds and squirrels—and Tristan. Tristan admired Zeno's quickness immensely, as one could see by his rapt attention to his friend, his eyes following Zeno's flight as though Zeno were a low-zooming bird. Zeno no doubt felt the approval and admiration. Cats recognize abilities, and moods. Tristan knew Zeno was fond of him, and the feeling was reciprocated, for whatever reason. It just was. For each, there was a comfort and peace and distinct pleasure in knowing and seeing and being in the presence of the other cat. It was perhaps a kind of love. Brotherly.

So, now a nice-sized family lived together happily on Grover Street. Wilma, Josh, humans; Lucky and Speeds, canines; Tristan and Zeno, felines. Their community was very mixed, consisting of cardinals, blue jays, mockingbirds, turtledoves, woodpeckers, golden finches, red-breasted finches, starlings, Brewer's blackbirds, house sparrows, wrens, tits, (many more birds), bats,   box turtles in hidden places, rabbits, groundhogs, raccoons, opossums,   gray squirrels, brown squirrels, moles, toads, frogs, boxers, bassets, poodles, cairn, shepherds, (and other breeds) and cats, cats, and cats galore; caterpillars, butterflies, potato bugs, ladybugs, cellar bugs, earwigs, ants (warriors and drones and queens), carpenter bees, mason bees, honey bees, sweat bees, wasps, dirt daubers, yellow jackets, snakes, lizards, spiders. Oh . . . so very many, flying, crawling, slithering, hopping, walking. Living together in town.

Tragedy

Zeno greatly disliked being taken off the property. When he had an appointment with the vet, he knew beforehand. He sensed the tension and even heard certain sounds that warned him: whispering, his name spoken with extra care or a dip of the voice or with a dart look at him, the very word "vet." It was a short, harsh word. He could hear it anywhere. But he by nature never revealed how much he understood. Even if his name were called, he might look the opposite direction for a short time, and then casually turn toward the speaker. Timing was a matter of the moment. This time it might take thirty seconds to turn. The next time he might have to clean his paw first. Cats understood the meaning of these delays. Humans can only guess or interpret from experience with their own cats. When Zeno heard "vet," he would stay in place for a while, perhaps looking downward, or even closing his eyes. But his mind was on walking away quietly and staying completely out of sight. In a few minutes, he would do just that. He had learned to look for the cat-carry if he passed through the garage or was in the basement for any reason. The cat-carry was always in one of those places, and if not, then it might be in the house, hidden, to be brought out for him. He would stay gone if the cat-carry wasn't in place. He couldn't outlast his humans, though. He needed a home, a house. And Tristan didn't mind the presence of the cat-carry. Tristan, truly, didn't mind much. He was a placid creature. Being near him was calming for Zeno.

Josh and Wilma decided to take a weekend trip. They worried mostly about Zeno.

"We could board the dogs, but leave the cats," Wilma said. "We can put enough food and water in the garage for two days, and extra on the deck."

"I imagine Zeno would like that."

"You know he would. He'll be better here. Nothing will hurt him. He has Tristan."

"We need a cat door, Wilma. If we fixed one of the windows for a cat entrance, we'd never have to worry about the cats. They could get away from anything and have shelter, food."

"Yes," Wilma said, not truly agreeing, "and we would be inviting every other outside animal to come roaming through the house. We can't do that."

"Lots of people do. And Lucky and Speeds wouldn't let anything in."

"If they were outside, and we were gone, anything could get on the deck and into the house."

"We could leave the gate . . ."

"See how complicated it's getting?"

Though they weren't angry, the tension in their voices had worried the pets. Zeno was standing by the kitchen door, nose close to the tiny opening between door and jamb, as if he could already smell the outside. By the time Josh reached the door, Zeno was standing on his hind legs and reaching for the knob, as if he could turn it. Possibly he was just showing Josh that he understood the function of the knob and the nature of the door. He was smart, and no one knew how much he truly understood. They were planning something, and it wasn't good for cats like Zeno, who need a family to be constant.

Handsome Tristan emerged from under the sideboard and reached the door in time to slink out before Josh closed it.

"I love these cats," Josh said. "They time everything to keep you off guard."

Two days later, after putting much food out for Zeno and Tristan, Wilma and Josh took the dogs away in the car and they didn't come back. In the morning that wasn't too strange or bad, though Zeno liked best when the dogs were properly in the back yard. Especially Speeds. She often smelled him, both rear and front, and occasionally licked one of his ears, just a quick, light flick upward on the outside part of his ear. It meant something. It brought a different feeling into Zeno's body. Not fear. His body recalled vaguely a box of small kittens like himself, and a tongue cleaning them all in gentle and rough flicks, sometimes turning him over. Pleasantly tumbling.

By evening, the empty house was too big, as if another house had slipped into the old one's spot. Zeno was uneasy. He was on the railing, but no one brought a saucer. Food left over from morning was in a saucer on the deck floor and a little pile was on the railing corner behind him. But a bird had been there, and now Tristan was watching the bird. When the bird darted away,

Tristan blinked slowly at Zeno and after a while, Zeno blinked back twice and turned his head away. He could feel Tristan's presence.

He walked down the stair railing, entered the garage through the doggy door. He was adept at pushing aside the rubber shield, as the dogs did, though it was heavy for him, and sometimes slapped against his side.

He stood in the shadows, smelling the always scent of the dogs but also their immediate absence. They weren't here.

A visible shudder went through his slender white frame.

He sat down. The dogs should be here. He turned his fine head toward the stairs to the dining room. He went to that door, sniffed along the bottom of it, returned to the garage floor. He hunkered down, closed his eyes. A thin green carpeting covered the floor, which might have been better than cement on his legs, but the carpet seemed to creep and he rose again, went to the basement steps, down, and poked only his head through the doggy door there. Dark and musty. The basement's back room would have crickets and spiders and dark underplaces, boxes, and space behind filing cabinets, and flat hiding slots under pallets. He didn't care about any of it. His green eyes were a little wild, and his movements faster. He withdrew his head and trotted up the basement steps and through that doggy door into the early dark evening. He headed for the rear gate. He knew Tristan was behind him somewhere, up on the deck, but walking was necessary right now. He had already walked twice, but he had to walk again, and to smell for the dogs. He was looking for Speeds. His tail went up and he walked faster than usual. All along his private route his nostrils flared and his tail had a nervous swag. If he had caught a scent of Speeds or Lucky, he might have varied his path and have gone after them. Now he turned corners, moved to rough sidewalk, paced on, on, around another corner. In his cat mind he surely thought that the house would be right again when he came back to it, that a dog named Speeds would be fidgeting about something, and Lucky would be observing. Speeds and Lucky. And the two humans. Wilma. Josh.

As Zeno passed the street entrance to his alley way, he looked almost down it, so quickly, as if he could have gone that route, and would be at his own back gate. He didn't. He would finish this route, this path, and come back to where he started. The house would be as it had been. He would take his place and have a saucer in front of him.

Just before he slid down between the gate posts, he glanced up. He didn't see Tristan on the railing. He pulled on through with a shadowy memory of Arthur threatening, and walked steadily to the back of the house. Still no Speeds. No Lucky. Leap to the stair railing, up it, curve around, slip between two slats. No Tristan. Up to the railing. Food still in corner. He sat, head up, green eyes noting everything in the evening dark yard. The yard light came on. This had happened before, but never with everyone gone. It was unnerving. He didn't quiver or start. Turning his head slowly and even pausing to scratch with teeth a spot on his left haunch, he sought Tristan. He sought him with eyes, ears, and nose. He sat erect for a while, and places floated through his mind, like thoughts, places for Tristan to be. He went to the corner where Tristan had been sitting earlier. He sniffed the blue peeling paint closely and followed the warmest scent of Tristan. With his head down, his body a bit lower, earnestly following Tristan's moves, he had to jump down to the deck, because Tristan's scent had stopped. Tristan had jumped somewhere. He found it at the edge of the deck, and along it, even on the slats. On the deck gate bottom. Between gate slats, heavy scent, as if Tristan had hung on the board for a long time. Zeno crawled over the board too, though he didn't like that exit. Sometimes the deck gate would not remain still but would swing with the cat strung over it. That was a way to avoid. But now he went through and the scent was again heavy to his left, to the bottom, and to the rear door and the doggy door. Zeno didn't hesitate. He followed Tristan's scent quickly, under and against that doggy door's slapping rubber into the garage. He saw Tristan. To the far side of the garage, beside a long board, a light-colored board, so Tristan's pattern of light and dark made a strange shape, long and unnatural. But Zeno didn't let that deter him. He went straight to his friend, his kinsman, his brother, his family closeness one. Tristan was not moving. Zeno sat down, head up. In a few seconds he looked down and bent, nudging Tristan's big chin and the side of his face. Tristan smelled different. Like Tristan but not warm. Not warm enough. Zeno meowed. It was a soft meow. Then another. He nudged Tristan again. He understood, without words, maybe without concepts humans would recognize, that the loss was complete and great and unfathomable and forever and more than he could bear. He made no sound for a long time. He nudged the dead body again and then again. He emitted one of the hollow, painful cries that meant all words.

He hunkered down by the body. He didn't nudge it again or meow. He didn't sleep. When morning came and the sun came up and no other being was in his house or his heart he went through the doggy door to the deck. He drank water. He ate one piece of dry cat food. He went along the railing, down the stair railing, down the yard, to the gate. Under it. To the left, tail up. To the right down to the alley.

When Zeno was a few yards away, sparrows alighted along the fence. A blue jay landed on the deck railing and ate rapidly a few pieces of cat food. The little dog chained on the corner yelped, but a kind of token yelp. The big brute just watched Zeno. Something was up. Something was different. Didn't everyone in the neighborhood know it? Wasn't it terrible? Something had happened that was changing a little world and they all felt a kind of loss even if a kind of threat had gone too. Pain was pain. A piece of white pain shaped like a cat was walking out the part of earth he had to live in.

Toward evening of the next day, Josh and Wilma arrived home. The house seemed quiet and empty because they had come too late to pick up Speeds and Lucky at the boarding kennel.

"We should have left earlier," Wilma said. "You think they know we're in town? Can they sense us from there?"

"Who knows what they sense." He whistled, twice, called, "Speeds! Lucky!" He winked at Wilma. "We'll see you in the morning."

"Wicked!" Wilma said, but she laughed. "I bet they heard you."

Zeno had heard the truck when it turned into their neighborhood and had heard the voices and the whistling and the calls. He had slunk off the railing and under the deck, up against the outer wall of the basement. Behind him was a window, small and very old and dirty, that had been set there years before, for circulation. Someone had tugged it partly out and he could push his way inside if he wanted to. He didn't. He listened to the movements of Wilma and Josh. He knew which part of the house they were in. When the kitchen door opened, Josh was right above him. "Hey, you guys!"

Josh's steps creaked across the deck. He was at the railing. "Zeno! Yo! Tristan! We're home!" He whistled. Zeno turned his head, cocked it down. He listened as if Tristan too listened and the pair of them were wary of what Josh would find. There was guilt to be felt and to be assigned. Zeno was angry at everyone, including himself. He was agitated even toward the ground and had to shift his weight and move a few inches this way, and then creep a few inches toward the yard. The next thing to do and the place to go weren't known yet. Josh skipped down the deck stairs and put his keys into the back door of the garage. Zeno's ears were pricked. A light switch clicked. Zeno stared at the ground.

Zeno heard a grunt, then walking, then a mumbling human voice, then "Oh no. Oh no." Zeno spun and dashed out the near side of the underdeck, leapt smoothly to the top of the post against the house, and was down, fleeing like a frightened ghost alongside the house and across the street to the schoolyard, which was a strange place, a long building with a hundred windows on the bottom floor and on the next, and two huge, huge trees that shadowed even in night the sloping yard. He could see the house across, where the woman and man lived, and where Lucky and Speeds were gone. And Tristan was there but gone. He walked to the concrete steps, wide ones, leading down to the street. He sat in the middle of one, a lorn cat looking at his former home. Night traffic with yellow and white and blue lights flowed along on the main street far to his right. Before him, only a car every now and then. The moon above was just a curved sliver, very orange. The neighborhood trees were clumps of round shadows under the blue-black sky. That white cat—in the midst of it, silent and waiting.

Josh was in the garage, squatted down by Tristan. He was talking on the telephone to the vet.

"Well, I'd like to bring him out there now. We don't want to keep him here like this until morning. It's got to upset Zeno. No telling where he is." He looked around, as if trying to find his white cat, and then said, "Okay. In a few minutes," and put away his phone.

Wilma had been in the basement and came up those stairs into the garage, carrying a box and a thin yellow blanket. "What'd they say? Can we bring him out?" Her voice was thick and her eyes were a little puffy and her lashes wet.

"Yes. He says he may not be able to tell us anything tonight, but he'll keep him for us and check him out in the morning."

Wilma started crying again, not loud. Her lips trembled and a few tears dampened her cheeks. "We can wrap him in this," she said, and knelt down by the handsome cat, too quiet now, gone wherever cats gather after here. She laid the small blanket over him and picked him up, tucking the blanket around him gently. "Did you see any mark on him?"

Josh shook his head no. "If he got into poison, then Zeno may have gotten it, too. I'm going to look for him."

"I don't want to take Tristan to the vet by myself."

"Okay. We'll go out there first, and then I'll look for Zeno."

When they were getting in the truck, Josh stopped and whistled, called "Zeno! Zeno! Hey, fellow. Come on home." He stayed quiet, listening and looking. "Zeno? It's okay."

Across the street, Zeno had moved to behind one of the tree trunks. When the man and woman left, he walked in his straight, steady fashion to the house and climbed into the back yard and into the garage. Gone. All of Tristan gone. Zeno sat on his haunches. He sniffed the place where Tristan had lain. He looked around the room, went down to the basement. Gone. Maybe he thought Wilma and Josh had done this. All the animals were gone but him. He remembered being the only one. He remembered another time. He went out into the night and across the street again and behind that tree. He knew that tree now and had lain there before. Someone came down the sidewalk and sat on the broad steps. It was a young man talking on his phone. He lighted a cigarette and Zeno could smell the heat and the tobacco, strange smell, in this territory. New.

"I don't see any injury at all," the vet said. "It could be poison. He wasn't dehydrated. I just don't know. I'm sorry, though. I know how you feel about your animals."

He was a very tall man, with a smooth, easy voice, and a kind tone. Animals liked him and so did their owners. He always wore jeans and plaid shirts, and he had a cowlick where the hair grew in a circle and wouldn't lie down. Right at the forehead his hair curled up and backward a little, maybe because he combed it that way, and thus he had a boyish look about him.

"I'll let you know in the morning," he said. "What do you want me to do with him afterward?"

At first Josh and Wilma didn't understand what the vet meant. This was the first pet each had lost and their parents had been the ones to hear such words.

"Oh," Wilma said. "I guess we want . . . Cremated?" She looked at Josh.

"Yeah," he said.

"Okay."

They looked at Tristan one more time, and each stroked him as if Tristan could feel it. "I hate this," Wilma said as they went out into the night air. "Hate it, hate it, hate it." Her nose was stuffy, but the words seemed just sad to Josh, not odd at all.

"I know. So do I."

They didn't bring Lucky and Speeds home from the kennel because what if some kind of poison or just a mean animal or person was near their house? They'd bring their other creatures home when they knew what happened to Tristan and that everyone was safe. They didn't feel safe themselves. When they parked the truck, they didn't want to go in the house. They roamed the neighborhood, calling "Zeno!"

"Zeno!" They called rather softly because they didn't want to disturb everyone. Dogs barked anyhow. At the old woman's shed which they knew was for all cats, they lingered, whispering "Zeno." They saw several cats, one of which was willing to rub against them and maybe go home with them, but they shied away. They passed their own house a few times, in case Zeno had come back. Two hours looking, when they were already tired, and were suffering a shock to their hearts.

Zeno heard them. But in his understanding they had taken Tristan, Speeds, and Lucky. When the house lights had gone completely dark, he went to the deck and ate a few dry bits of food, then he left by his usual way and walked far, far down the alley, past everything he knew. He could smell water and the denseness of many trees and damp soil, and he headed resolutely in that direction. He was crossing a well-traveled north and south road and moving into the heavy brush and trees and sloping yards down to Bear Creek. Many creatures lived there. He was very visible and messages passed along the creature line about that white cat, the skinny one. Something was wrong with him. Cat and not cat.

The vet phoned. Tristan had likely died from heart disease, something he had had all along. Maybe a sudden exertion. There were no external injuries and no sign of poison. Was that better to know? Maybe. Still, Tristan had been alone. And so had Zeno, at such a terrible time. They had to find Zeno.

Josh put an ad in the Lost Pets column of the paper and he and Wilma taped "lost cat" flyers wherever allowed and a few places where they weren't certain a sign was allowed. They knocked on doors up and down their street and nearby ones, describing Zeno. Many people already knew him by sight but hadn't seen him recently.

Lucky had a sense of the situation. He had smelled the patch of indoor-outdoor carpeting where death had actually occurred. He smelled the trace of Zeno. He kept a sharp lookout for Zeno though he understood in his own way that Tristan was gone not to come back—dogs and cats likely have no concept of forever except that the missing one will not come back. That's enough to know. Speeds, however, was quietly frantic. She was always an agitated dog, wanting to fulfill her duties and not having any other way than staying as close to Wilma or Josh as possible, to come quickly if called. She also took care of the water dish. If it was empty she would stand by it for a while and if no one filled it, she would grasp the edge of it in her mouth and carry it to the closest human, Josh or Wilma, and drop it at that person's feet. When they had used a plastic water dish, this duty had been simple, but with so many pets drinking, they had one huge metal bowl in the kitchen, by the sideboard. When it was empty—Lucky drank a lot of water—Speeds had to tug it and for the last few feet could lift it only by throwing her head back and kind of staggering toward Josh or Wilma.

Without Zeno, Speeds felt she had seriously neglected a duty and was neglecting it still. The house was agitated, too, through the voices and movements of Josh and Wilma. When Speeds tried to rest, she expected the white cat to come beside her, at least once. It was gone. Speeds got on the sofa one afternoon, sort of deliberately, and lay on her side, head up a little. This was what Zeno liked. To come lie against her and to clean his paws and chest and rub wet paws against his eyes. He would eventually fall asleep and Speeds would, too, dozing, though, like a mother with a pup. She knew this was no pup. She was not confused. She was simply motherly and recognized she had been assigned a role. Speeds accepted roles. Now she lay there hoping Zeno would come.

Five days and not a sign of Zeno. The weather turned colder, and rain sluiced down again, and both Josh and Wilma had to fight away thoughts of Zeno having another rough time, of him being hungry and out in the weather, and lost. Or dead. Long gone to them.

"He loved Tristan, you know," Wilma said.

"Of course I know. What you know about him, I know about him. I just don't want to talk about it. I'd rather deal with it at a distance, as much as I can."

On the eighth day, when Josh answered the house phone, he heard a male voice. "I think I know where your cat is."

"Where? I can't believe it. Where?"

Wilma had come to attention. Her heartbeat quickened. "What is it?"

Josh waved her quiet, picked up a pencil and the message pad. "What's the address? Could you show us where you've seen him? Okay! Okay! Tomorrow morning. Is 8:00 okay? Seven? That's even better. Thank you so much."

He turned even as he was putting the phone back into the base. "This guy has seen Zeno. He's showing up in the same place every day. He's doing that walking bit. We'll get him." He nodded. "Tomorrow. I'd like to go over there right now, but I'm afraid we'd scare him off."

Wilma wanted to know the address and she got out the city map and read the streets. She took some frozen baked chicken from the freezer and left it out to thaw.

Next morning, the man who had seen Zeno willingly guided Wilma and Josh up the alley that ran behind the houses on his block, some facing east, some west. Streetlights were still on and cast a little foggy light over the deep yards. Almost all of them were unfenced, but had rock gardens, or landscaping, sheds or decks or cars—something to hide in and behind. The alley ended on the north side at a rough-ground patch, hilly and rocky. It had been filled with trash and then packed with dirt. Now it was sodden and dismal, with clumps of dead weeds like huge spiders everywhere.

"It's terrible," Wilma said. "Zeno!" She looked a little wild herself, without a hat, rain slicking her dark hair straight around her face. Josh put his arm over her shoulder. "We'll find him." He turned to the man. "How many times have you seen him?"

"Maybe three. No, four. My wife saw him, too. He cuts through here. I think if you can wait around, you'll see him. If not, I'll get him for you when I can."

"He might run from you and change his route," Josh said. "He likes patterns." He looked at Wilma as if to confirm what he said, being surprised a little that he knew that about Zeno. He hadn't articulated it aloud before.

The man had to go to work, and though Josh needed to open the music store, he called the young man who gave guitar lessons there and asked him to open up. He had a key.

The rain continued, slow and steady and dreary, but the wind let up. The couple crossed that muddy lot, stepped when they could on clumps of weeds, but even doing so, wound up muddy past the ankles and fairly chilly. At the edge of the trees and undergrowth lining Bear Creek, they split up and walked along the tree line, calling "Zeno? Zeno?" in their softest tone but loud enough for him to hear.

And hear them he did. He was out of the rain, tucked back into a kind of natural rock grotto in the upper bank across the creek. He was lying on his stomach, semi-dozing, when he heard them first approaching and the voices brought a feeling of turmoil, a kind of hurt throughout himself. He looked at the ground by his paws, seemingly engaged in something tiny there, but he was listening. Wilma's voice said a word he recognized. "Chicken." It was two syllables, had a distinct sharp sound followed by a soft one. The sound in her voice meant a particular food. He remembered Tristan eating chicken. Zeno got up at the memory and turned to look the other way, as if he were only rearranging his position more comfortably. He didn't want to leave the grotto but he would if that discomfort continued to call. He lay more fully on his belly, stretching his neck and laying his head on his forearms, a little to one side. He closed his eyes. Not a sleeping cat at all, though he looked to be.

Wilma continued going back during daytime, walking up the alley with a little zip package of chicken. She had placed jar lids at each end of the alley and had put chicken in them. The chicken was always gone, but she didn't believe Zeno was the cat who got it. She thought that if he were alive, and he heard her voice, he would come. Didn't he love her and

Josh? Certainly he did. Poor frightened, hard-luck cat. Poor Zeno. And poor Wilma. When she went home that last evening, she was trying to convince herself not to come back. She even had a cold from traipsing around in the wet weather, calling, standing and waiting. Josh had done much the same, only he often drove around the new neighborhood. He would ask any person he saw if they had seen a thin white cat during the past two weeks. Twice the answer was yes, but the direction was where they had been looking. The last visit, he sat in the truck at the alley's end, hoping to see that white tail coming through the early dimness. He, like Wilma, was giving up hope, however much he didn't want to. He'd rather believe Zeno had found a place he liked better, a home where someone was there all the time but left him alone when he desired solitude. Josh closed his own eyes, took a deep breath and hoped deeply that when he opened them, he would see Zeno. "Please," he whispered.

It wasn't time yet.

At that capitulation, when they both had resigned themselves to the loss of Zeno, Speeds presented a solution. Perhaps it wasn't knowingly, since dog minds are mysteries in many ways, as are their many talents.

She wouldn't eat. Now, Speeds always ate. She didn't bolt her food—neither did Lucky— but she seemed to feel it was obligatory that she eat and that she look around to ensure that everyone was enjoying what they had. She would take a mouthful, raise her head as she chewed and look at Lucky and, if they were there, the cats. This morning she didn't eat. Instead, she went into the laundry room and looked up at the dryer. She lay down on the floor there, her bewilderment evident in her pert ears and her intense eyes. She made a sound much like a sigh, only at a very low pitch. Maybe a moan. She did that again. Wilma and Josh looked at each other.

"She's worried, too," Wilma said. "She's grieving."

"I wouldn't go that far." Josh looked at Speeds who emitted the sound again. "Well, maybe so."

"I'm going to take her over there," Wilma said, and got up immediately, going for her coat. "Zeno likes her. Maybe he's afraid of me, but he won't be afraid of her."

"He may not be there at all," Josh said. "Don't get your hopes up."

"I want to. One more day."

Speeds was ready, whether or not she understood what was actually happening. It was too early for the usual time of Zeno's path-walking. Wilma thought that might be good. She wanted to arrive before he struck out, so the whole path would be a possibility.

She put Speeds on a leash, which Speeds didn't like and shied away from, but finally permitted, since she was accustomed to obeying and even to anticipating an order. Wilma parked the car at the south end of the alley, but as she stepped onto that rougher roadway, she changed her mind. She turned to her right instead, and took the sidewalk, going on the resident front side of the block. She walked slowly and paused often, peering closely at a house front, porch, sides, shrubs. At the north end, she crossed over, by the empty lot. She scanned that area, seeking something very white, maybe scrunched down small. Nothing. She looked also down the alley, which she had walked so many days. Maybe she and Josh had frightened Zeno away from the alley. She didn't call him. She didn't talk to Speeds. She went on past the alley, across a yard with railroad-tie flowerbeds, empty now, and white plastic storage containers under the deck. She felt she was on the right track and was afraid to think about it, because she might jinx it.

On that west sidewalk there were many houses, and beyond them another street and more houses. That would mean much traffic, but also many places to hide quickly. Speeds was tugging just enough to keep the leash a bit taut, which was her way, but she also looked around and paused now and then, not sniffing the ground, peering, listening. Her sharp ears were up. Wilma stopped and just let Speeds move around at the end of the lead space. If Speeds went into a yard, Wilma followed a little. They were angling back to the sidewalk, so they could avoid a pile of lumber, old lumber, different lengths and shades, with nail holes and knot holes, and dark markings of numbers, when, from behind it, slowly and easily, came Zeno. Wilma stood still though it took such willpower not to call Zeno or attempt to scoop him up and race to the car with him. She let him greet the now trembling Speeds, who glanced at Wilma repeatedly at first, as if asking is this all right? Is this what I should do?

Wilma didn't know how to get Zeno home. Should she walk to the car and hope he followed? If he didn't, she could bring Speeds back. Should she try to coax Zeno to her? Should she sit down in the damp yard? He would never get in the car voluntarily. If she picked him up, he might fight her and get more frightened. She wasn't going to scare him, no matter what.

"Come on Speeds," she said, and Speeds, looking first at Zeno, then Wilma, slowly started off. Zeno followed, very near, as if he would stroke Speeds with his body. So Wilma didn't rush them and stopped often. When they reached the car, the test presented itself. Would Zeno come with them? She unhooked Speeds' leash. She opened the rear passenger door. Speeds hesitated but leapt in. Zeno was on the curb soil, standing, tail up but unmoving. Wilma didn't speak. Speeds was panting but seated mid-seat, looking out at Zeno.

Zeno leapt inside. Wilma closed the door.

At home, Wilma carried him from the car and he didn't struggle. He was a bit rigid as if he'd leap from her arms at the slightest opportunity, but she clung with her left arm while she opened the door, and then loosened her hold and he leapt cleanly to the wood floor of the house. His house. She was astonished that he strode into the kitchen as if he hadn't been gone, hadn't been afraid of her, hadn't caused such desperation for ten days. But she didn't care. She was joyous. She phoned Josh and exclaimed briefly while following Zeno into the kitchen. He had jumped onto the sideboard—a definite NO—but Wilma didn't speak harshly. She picked him up gently, put him on the floor, murmured "sweet little guy" and "dear cat" and "foolish boy" while she got cream out of the refrigerator and poured a saucer full and put it on the dryer. While he was up there, she defrosted more chicken in the microwave, watched closely and hopefully by both Speeds and Lucky who were in the dining room.

"Chicken for everyone," she said, waving her right hand happily. "All creatures." She caught herself and said low, "Except chickens and fowl of course."

She called their veterinarian and asked him to please make a house call. He had done it before when she once thought Speeds had been injured and was lying dead in the back yard. Speeds had only caught her collar on a fallen small branch and was somehow pinned by the way she lay on the branch. Moving choked her a bit so she lay perfectly still.

The vet had been so amused—relieved

and amused—and Wilma had been fond of him ever since. He thought her fear of looking at Speeds' injury was admirable. She had been crying when he arrived. She was smiling when he left. Embarrassed but happy.

Now she needed him to check over their Zeno without too much stress. Zeno had been through a lot.

That wasn't true in Zeno's perception. The days he had spent were another experience that his body knew—discomfort but fortitude, survival, knowledge, resources. His world had expanded. It wasn't all pleasant. It wasn't the world he had once known as a kitten and sometimes dreamed about even when waking, but it was a world he knew better than he had and better than many cats. He had seen strange cats in those ten days but had avoided any frightening encounters. There was a beauty in the rushing water he had crossed on a log, and the rivulets of rain down branches and splatters in the muddy banks, and in the hoots and caws and shrieks and darts of a creek world. He liked it. He had seen Speeds and wanted that sight and smell and company and comfort. He was drawn to her. It was good to stay with her. And safe. And good to be in this high warm place, with smells he knew, and no harm, no hiding.

He fought the veterinarian only lightly. He knew the man. Speeds was watching. Zeno went still, let the man press and probe and look in his mouth.

"He's a pretty cat," the vet said. "I'm taking a few samples, and if he needs anything, we'll let you know. I think he's okay." He ruffled Zeno's head as if Zeno were a dog. "Had some adventures, did you?"

"We can't give him pills," Wilma said. "So if he needs medication, could you come by with a shot?"

"Yep. Can do."

When the vet left, Lucky got in the big doggy bed. Speeds lay down on a throw rug near the piano in the dining room. Zeno lay down on the rug, too, back against Speeds' legs. Zeno slept a long time or seemed to. Speeds woke and stayed there until she couldn't bear it and tried to get up. Zeno moved to the living room sofa and slept alone, curled tightly.

Zeno woke when Josh came home. He could hear Josh and Wilma talking. He smelled kitty litter and heard the rustle of the bag. They were fixing it for him. He heard water being poured into the water dish. He kept his eyes shut. He remembered Tristan and Arthur and cats before them. A big dog. A huge bird in the sky. A man in a field. His own running, running, running, running.

A Sweet Time

The back yard became well grassed each summer. Trees lushed out and bird feeders hung here and there through the neighborhood. Squirrels ran madly along limbs and lines and gutters and roofs. Opossums climbed into attics and had their babies, and groundhogs dug tunnels under houses. Birds and rabbits pecked strawberries and blackberries and raspberries. Honeysuckle vines crept through vine beds and surprise flowers popped up everywhere. Some summers were so wet the house basement held puddles of water, and some were so dry the ground cracked. The skies were marvelous, sometimes blue and wide, sometimes black and roiling; clouds sailed the sunset colors, yellow, amber, red, lavender, purple, gold, blue, and the upper world seemed a wonderland of soaring life.

Zeno resumed his path with only slight

variation. He met Arthur alone one afternoon when he was shortly back from the first adventure. Zeno walked right past Arthur, expecting to be slammed sharply from the rear, above his tail. Expecting it and walking on was his bravery. This was his to do—walk here. Arthur had a sense of what Zeno felt. He was a cat, too, and he could read that assurance and odd strength, the willingness to be threatened and to survive the attack. He remembered the gray who had befriended Zeno. That had been a very brave and big cat. So Arthur watched Zeno and didn't feel rage or insult. He walked after him a little but became bored and turned back. He was an old cat, anyhow, and not too interested in fighting. He liked watching fights better.

A strange cat appeared in the alley, sitting just outside the fence. Beyond him, as backdrop, was the dark green garbage bin. His color stood out against that darkness and the plum tree trunks inside the fence. Josh saw him, because he sometimes parked the truck in back.

"There's a huge cat watching our place," he told Wilma. "He may be after Zeno."

"Maybe he's just hungry."

"Don't feed him," Josh said, knowing that

she would. Wilma fed creatures. She didn't want anything to be hungry.

"If I feed the stray cats," she said, "they'll leave the birds alone."

"No they won't. Hunting birds is natural to them. If you want them not to hunt, you have to make them housecats. All of them."

Wilma put a small pile of dry cat food outside the fence, and down the alley, not near their gate, sort of on the edge of the alley. She put an old, shallow cake pan at the edge of the parking lot and filled it with water.

Zeno saw the orange cat. It was tall, thin, and battered. It stared fixedly at Zeno when Zeno was on the deck but wasn't seen anywhere when Zeno walked.

"It's on the deck," Josh told Wilma as he came home one evening. "That orange bruiser. That is one big cat. He's friendly, too."

"He's on the deck?"

"Yeah. And so's Zeno. Apparently, they hit it off. Maybe Zeno will have another friend." He opened the kitchen door so she could see and they both watched quietly. Zeno was to the left on the corner of the railing, and the orange was to the right on a corner. The orange one was looking at Josh and Wilma, but Zeno was staring at the orange. His face was stoic, his eyes placid, but they knew. Something about the tail.

"Zeno's afraid," Wilma said.

"I think you're right. We have a problem. Let Lucky and Speeds out."

Josh went out the door to carry Zeno in but Zeno jumped from the railing to the ground and walked to the gate. The orange jumped down, too. So Josh just skittered down the steps, swooped up Zeno before he could get through the gate-post gap. Lucky came like a low-running wolf toward the orange who stopped, his back against the fence, hissed, and when Josh said, "Okay, Lucky. Okay," the cat sprang toward and ran up the nearest plum tree and dropped over the fence.

"I wish Zeno would fight!" Josh said. "He's really a cowardly cat." Zeno was squirming, but Josh held him fast. Inside the house, he released him. "Maybe we should let him get beat up. Maybe he'd learn to fight."

"He can't," Wilma said. "It's too late. Some animals can't fight back and he's one of them."

"I guess I know that. I just don't want it to be true. I'd teach him if I knew how. We could make him a housecat, keep him in."

Wilma laughed, not mean spirited, just at

the idea that Zeno, who had to walk his heart out, could be kept inside. "We'd be the death of him."

"Maybe not. He might get used to it and have a long, safe, healthy life."

"If we have to do that, we will."

The orange stayed away.

There were other bullies. An orange tabby who had a gash across the back of his neck, a wide gash, still bloody, and Zeno could smell it. At night, when Josh and Wilma were oblivious inside or in bed, the tabby would take to the railing and eat whatever was left. Zeno let him have the railing. One night Zeno escaped into the garage and then down into the basement, but the tabby came after him, back to where the pipes came down from the upstairs bathroom, long pipes wrapped in rags, going underground. That underpart was mostly packed dirt, no hiding place. Zeno had backed against the sandstone wall and waited. When the tabby came closer, Zeno held his place, then darted just as the cutting swipe came, so it missed him and he was streaking across the basement and flying through the basement doggy door up cement steps, out the garage doggy door into the night and away, away. The tabby came after him but stopped mid-yard, probably hurting and needing help himself. Zeno found one of his escape spots, not comfortable, and closed his eyes, hunkered down, finally slipping into sleep, ears still awake.

Wilma had seen that stranger cat and had Animal Control come take him away. She felt guilt. Would the animal-control staff treat and heal an old unneutered cat? She paid a no-kill fee so they'd keep the tabby alive and send him to another shelter in the city.

Other mean or competitive cats assessed the white one, Zeno, and went after him, and thus Zeno had a few scars. He had a small split in the edge of one ear, a tiny curve missing from the other, a few shallow puncture scars. He never vigorously fought back in cat fights. They weren't really fights. They were attacks and escapes. Unfortunately, he was used to being set apart by one of his own kind, and targeted. He took the role, not having another. His wounds were small, but they hurt as did the thought of their being inflicted. But these experiences were of one cloth to Zeno. They were part of life. His life. He feared, he was hurt, and he healed, alone. Alone as far as he knew. But in between, he was free.

Zeno was so quick. White and fast and predictable. Students who lived in small rentals in the area expected to see him at about the same time daily. They admired him, the clean lines and steady pace. They thought probably no one messed with him. They thought he was the boss cat of the neighborhood.

Josh once wanted to bathe Zeno. The downstairs bathroom was off the laundry room. A white shower fit in the bathroom corner, with a rounded, gliding, clear bubbly-plastic door. Josh had the shower door open, the warm water spraying fine against the inner shower wall. He picked up Zeno in the kitchen and made it through the laundry room and to the bathroom door. Zeno caterwauled and caught claws into the door jamb, and then into the shower door, tugging, shriek-meowing, and scratching wildly with his rear feet. It might have appeared funny, but for Josh and Zeno it was misery. Josh had deep scratches on left biceps and a three-stripe scratch across his abdomen, not too deep, but bleeding still. Wilma caught Zeno in the study, pulling him from beneath the daybed and throwing a towel over him, crunching him to her.

He would not soothe. Would not. She let him flee into the cat-carry and put it on the deck, grate door open, so he could sneak away freely.

Wilma bathed and medicated Josh's wounds. She didn't want Josh to be angry. She didn't want to lose Zeno. She needn't have worried. Josh didn't want to lose Zeno either.

"Why doesn't he fight cats like that?" Josh said. "He's got the strength, I tell you that. I think he could've pulled the whole shower from the wall."

"He wasn't trying to hurt you," Wilma said. "He hurt you getting away. Cats have the same claws he does, and they *are* out to hurt him."

"Yeah. I know. You think I might get cat fever?"

"Maybe."

He didn't, though he could have.

Zeno was a clean cat and bathed often, but sometimes he came home scruffed up. Other times he came in completely dusty and Wilma knew why. He would roll and squirm into dry dust, deliberately, in the alley or in a bare spot in the yard. Roll, squirm. It was a natural way to fight skin parasites, such as fleas, but Zeno didn't have fleas or any other skin affliction

100

she could see. He was treated regularly by Josh, just as the dogs were, to keep him healthy. It required only holding him a few seconds and squirting a liquid medication against skin at the shoulder-neck line. Josh could do it in one sweep. Zeno rolled because it was one of his pleasures, a cat activity he had seen or was born wanting to do. Maybe he had learned it from a dog. Not Speeds, who never once in her entire life deliberately got dirty.

When Wilma saw Zeno in one of his soiled states, she got out an old, soft washcloth and a bowl of warm water. Using only one finger wrapped in a corner of the damp cloth, she gently cleaned a small area. Zeno became accustomed to this and would accept more and more. By going slowly, with no rough or sudden moves, Wilma could clean that white hair and even the face. Zeno had a sweet face when he was allowing the cleaning.

"Don't tell anyone," she whispered to him. "I don't do this for every cat."

Zeno tolerated being petted but only around the head and in a straight line down the spine, and no extra rubbing. He would ease away, sometimes put teeth to hand, but not bite. He walk-stroked Speeds and sometimes did the same to Wilma's legs. Was he petting them or petting himself safely? It was surely affection. If, late at night, he couldn't go outside for whatever reason, he would feign sleep and later roam the house restlessly. He might emit a hollow cry which the others heard and raised their heads about but lay back down. Zeno. He might go into the bedroom where the humans slept. Perhaps he was hoping they would waken and let him outside. Perhaps he just wanted to be with them. Cats do love, though they may reveal it oddly. He may have been comforted by the two scents, male and female, the two biggest creatures in his family, the strongest. He would come up on the bed easily, because he weighed so little, tread and pinch at the covering and then settle down by one of them or between. He would rise before they did and be downstairs. He might nap by the food dish on the dryer or appear to nap. He was part of the family but weaving in and around it.

Josh began putting a towel on his side of the bed, at the foot. He shaped and patted it into a kind of circle with a recessed center, a little bed.

"You're wooing Zeno to your side," Wilma said.

"Yep."

"You love that cat."

"Yep. So do you."

Wilma nodded. 'Twas true.

Zeno would take naps on Josh's lap or Wilma's or lie by them on the sofa, but they couldn't move. If they moved too much, he was gone.

"I feel like a piece of furniture," Wilma said. "He can bathe while I'm napping, but I can't move if he's sleeping. I wonder if he loves us. You can tell with the dogs, but with Zeno, I don't know."

"I think he does. He just needs something we can't give him."

Seasons passed. Children from the schoolyard saw the white cat and he saw them. The street was broadened. Zeno grew older. He had patterns of movement and places to go and regular food and sleep. He had Speeds. Memories. He had been a kitten but not long enough. His body and mind remembered that as a loss.

The Adoption

A new dog was in the house, a puppy, named Lollygag by Wilma because of the animal's casual, lazy movements. When carried, Lollygag would twist to be on her back, able to see, and her very pink tongue would loll out one side of her mouth. She was a big puppy, though, almost the size of Speeds, and when grown would be at least the size of Lucky, maybe larger. The name was quickly shortened to Lolly. She had strange eyes, light brown and rather neutral. The lack of expression might have been hereditary but might have been because Lolly, even so young, knew she had to be humble—the older dog Speeds was the boss, and Lucky was also boss, almost equal to Speeds. Thus, Lolly was in last place. In human terms describing the social structure of canines, Speeds was the Alpha female, Lucky the Alpha male, and Lollygag the Omega female. Alpha and Omega, first and last.

Zeno stayed clear of the puppy. Canines might appear friendly when their owners were around, but they could be deceitful, even when puppies. Lolly would reveal her nature as animals do, so Zeno was cautious as he had learned to be. He observed Lolly from a higher spot such as the back of the sofa or a chair, or an upper stairstep. Outside, he looked for her presence before he entered the yard. Her nature seemed placid and slow. She wasn't very active and didn't move suddenly. He was far swifter. She observed her surroundings as he did, quietly. When leaves fell, she watched them drift down as if they were alive. If a butterfly fluttered in sight she watched as long as it was visible. If a beetle struggled across summer grass, she would walk nose-close, smelling the creature, yet never hurt it. She snapped only at flies, but did so quickly, jerking around as if they were tormenting her. Zeno didn't like flies either. With her almond eyes, Lolly acknowledged Zeno, but she never barked at him or teased him. Once she made a wet whuffing sound when he lowered his head to her food dish, just smelling. He wasn't worried. In the cat domain of the house, he was Alpha. Lolly wasn't for him but she wasn't *against* him.

Although Zeno didn't always recognize what was happening among the canines, repeated behavior trained him. He knew Lolly was bullied. She had to obey rules enforced by Speeds. Lolly could not get in front of Speeds. She would be corrected with a yap or snap or a secret look that a human might not see. If the canines were going upstairs to the bedroom, or downstairs, or out the door, or walking on a leash anywhere, Lolly had to be in the rear. She also could show no excitement. If she bounced around—frolicked—Speeds would bite at the curls on Lolly's neck and twist the curls so that Lolly was taken to the ground. If Lolly managed to stay up, because she became quickly a heavy dog and could have brought Speeds down, then Lucky would join in. He would nip at Lolly's ankles—he didn't break the skin, just threatened close. Lolly was not allowed to drink from the water dish before Speeds. She could not accept any succulent bite in Speeds' presence, even if Wilma or Josh handed it to her directly. If they put a bit of steak or pork in her mouth, she would let it fall. If they placed it before her on the deck or in her dish, she would walk away from it. They worried about the unfairness but even if they shut Speeds outside and tried to give Lolly a treat alone, the big girl wouldn't accept it. Animals have rules and reasons we can't always understand.

Zeno saw beyond the blandness in Lolly's eyes. She was free in her own way. Lolly would not smell Speeds' mouth. Dogs have a custom of allowing one another to smell their teeth, perhaps indicating what food has been eaten (or some other reason). Lolly wouldn't do it for Speeds. When Speeds paraded with a favorite toy, like a scepter, Lolly would not ask for it, would not even look at it. Nor would she grovel. Although she allowed herself to be dragged down by Speeds, she resisted *total* subservience, and Speeds accepted the resistance. And Lolly did feel fondness. She always sought to lie by Lucky in the sun or in the house, in much the comfortable way that Zeno and Tristan had enjoyed. Speeds would look longingly at the two.

When Josh took the dogs out in the truck and brought them back, sometimes Lolly would run for freedom instead of through the gate, ignoring Josh's yelling. She would bound along, along, ears flapping, happily away, big enough to be in the center of the alley. She always came back in about an hour, panting, wearing burrs and twigs and bits of leaf meshed and woven into her heavy fur. Joyous. She would flop down on her belly, still breathing heavily from her wild illicit run, eyes bland and passionless. The eyes were a lie. Lolly was behind there, full of life and love. Zeno sometimes sat close enough to show he felt safe in her presence, felt a same-family closeness, same-household, same-country.

Close to fondness.

The Ice Age

The rain began freezing by mid-morning. Bare trees glistened in the winter sun and for a while looked like glass. Then they whitened. Everything whitened and went still. Power lines were down, and as the day turned to late afternoon and evening and the temperature dropped, many homes had no heat, no lights, no hot water. People brought out emergency heat, such as kerosene heaters and butane heaters. Some homes had fireplaces and those lucky families gathered around that warmth, crawling into sleeping bags for the evening. Some people moved in with relatives or friends.

Zeno sat on the railing at the corner of the house, staring out at this new world. He was rather impervious to the cold, because actually freezing temperature wasn't that cold. Many, many, many times he had been in colder weather. It was the ice. He looked right and left, impassively, shifted his feet and scooted back, not from fear or cold. He blinked slowly. When he heard the kitchen door opening, he jumped down and went toward Wilma and the inner house, but he passed her instead, scooted through slats and down stairs, and sashayed on the ice toward the gate.

"Zeno!" Wilma called. "Come back here. Come on."

He heard her coming out and he hurried toward the gate gap. There wasn't room. It was filled higher and harsh, and he had to back away.

"Zeno. Come on, baby. We've got to go."

Her urgency disturbed him. He slowly walked diagonally toward the side of the house. The shreds of dry grass crackled and broke beneath his pads. A sharp sound snapped overhead and a branch fell beside him. He bolted toward the front fence, low, slipped only once.

"Zeno!"

He clawed over the fence, scraped his belly. The vines by the house were stiff. He continued steadily toward the front and sat on a step there. The school trees were ice. No children in sight. A car came by, the windows white with scraped-clear patches. White smoke

112

came out the back. The traffic light was dark. The sun was shining but silver. The light wasn't warm. It was time, though, for his first walk. He wasn't at ease but he had no choice. He struck out, going around the east side, down the length side of the backyard fence, into the alley.

He was seven years old now. Still very thin. He didn't have the sagging flesh at his loins that some older cats get. He looked like an Egyptian cat statue, only walking. Thin and white and purposeful.

Some neighbors saw him. They marveled at the strange cat who must be neurotic or brave or foolish. He didn't even pause much or digress. He didn't chase anything, not that anyone had seen him do. Just foot forward, foot forward, foot forward.

But ah, that foot forward felt good to Zeno. He could rely on his movement, leaving behind first one feeling, then another, then picking up a new one, leaving another behind. So he moved around and with his emotions, those he carried with him from his first breath outside his mother's body and those he had gained since then. His walking was a gift to himself, discovered by accident and by necessity.

Would he have liked to be inside,

sheltered, cozied up by a fire or lapping up cream? Probably not. The time for that was when his body felt it was the time for that. Now was walk.

Josh and Wilma didn't want to leave their companions alone, especially not just one of them. Speeds, they knew, would be best for Zeno. But Speeds was now twelve, which was pretty old for a dog her size. Her muzzle was more white and gray than black, and she didn't see as well or hear as well. She was definitely still boss. When the pets' supper was served, Speeds walked head up, barking, before she settled down to her own meal. She had always eaten standing up, but now she couldn't easily lower her head to the food dish without her legs sliding apart. So Wilma put an old throw rug down for Speeds to have dinner on. The rug kept her legs from slipping, and the dish, now set on top of a square pillow, was close to her mouth. She ate with gusto, checking quickly how the others were doing.

They couldn't leave Speeds with Zeno and Zeno wasn't going to come close to anyone in this time of strange cold and slickness. He had mastered walking on the ice. Of course, he had been on ice before, but not in a world of

114

it, trees and alley and every single thing frozen into itself and into the whole simultaneously, a meshing of ice. As it began thawing, it was treacherous anew. Crashes happened all the time, bits of trees. Black limbs laced the sky and sometimes a huge limb would fall into the road. The schoolyard was a maze of limbs.

Deciding the power had to be back on soon, Josh and Wilma, on the second cold day, left Lolly with Zeno—Lolly truly liked cold weather—and took Speeds and Lucky along to their friend's house. They left dry food high on a garage cabinet for Zeno and a big bowl of dry on the floor for Lolly.

Later, Zeno came through the garage doggy door and saw Lolly lying in her big bed which was usually upstairs in the house. She was in a loose curl, head resting on the raised side of the bed. She didn't lift her head though her eyes turned toward him. He sat where he was, studied Lolly as she studied him. Being alone together was new. In a little while, he walked to the cabinet, jumped in a smooth arc to the flat surface, and quietly began munching the dry food. He lay down next to the bowl, ignoring his own bed, and slept.

They both snored. Lolly had a bubble snore,

not loud. Zeno had the slightest whistle, faint, through his nostrils. It was rare that he made any sound at all while sleeping. The weaving snores were a pleasant duet.

They were wakened by a thick cracking and a crush rumble and a shaking of the garage roof. Both were out the doggy door in seconds, while fine slivers and dust of ice and tree bark and wood misted the air and wafted down to the deck and the ground. And the roof. The big tree by the deck had lost a huge limb, one that reached over the roof of the house. It had fallen over laundry and kitchen rooms, and part had broken off and down to the garage roof. The deck was a clutter of debris. Lolly ran up the deck stairs to look, and down and around, and then under the deck, and then back to the stairs. She had a lovely, brushy tail and it moved constantly now as she nosed around and looked around, oblivious to Zeno.

Zeno was tired. His was a brave heart, but this was his world and home and big changes had come one right after the other. He didn't think about fairness or concepts like earning rest or proving himself, but his body trembled a little, as if the muscles had run enough and here was another stretch of race. He went on his trek when it was time, head more down, but tail up, the tip crooked. He saw one cat down by the old shed. He wondered, cat fashion, if Arthur were gone.

When Wilma came that evening, into the house all cold and empty, she felt a fresh coolness and heard Lolly's greeting yelps from the garage. "Poor girl," she muttered. She hurried to open the door from dining room to garage and noticed, just out of the corner of her eye, sort of a sense or a hint, that something was wrong. But she swung open the door first and was met by a wet dog curving around her legs, a sweeping tail. "Okay, Lolly! Okay! Where's Zeno?" She peered down into the garage dimness. A few newspapers were scattered, blown from the recycle box. And the outside door seemed— crooked? Lopsided? Her memory of something amiss in the kitchen made her turn and hurry toward that doorway. The ceiling was dropping, broken, dripping, over the kitchen table. The laundry room, too, had dangling sharp boards, though the doorjamb between the two rooms seemed okay.

She was shocked breathless, brought her palm up to her chest. Lolly had come inside and now nosed around the kitchen floor, lapping water from the melted ice.

"No girl," she said, and went into the living room, calling Josh on her cell phone.

Together they took photos and called the insurance man and gathered up more belongings. They went out back, called Zeno and stood in the alley for a few minutes. The ice sparkled and still made crackling sounds.

"The town lost a lot of trees," Josh said. "It's going to look like wasteland when the ice is gone." He began calling again. "Zeno! Hey, old fellow! Come on."

Zeno was down by the cat woman's shed. He heard Josh and Wilma and he closed his eyes. He was comfortable just then, warm in the shed and in the scent of other cats for a long time. Through half dozing eyes he saw Arthur and a black cat, smaller, with small face and huge ears. The ears made Zeno open his eyes wider for a while. He heard his name a few times more. He thought of Lolly, the wide swath of her tail and her deep bark.

"We've never been able to take care of him," Josh said, closing Wilma's car door for her. "He's a neurotic cat. I don't know."

"The ice storm rattled him. He's okay. He'll come around."

"We could've packed him off to the vet, I

guess."

"He doesn't eat out there either."

Zeno ate a few pieces of dry from the old woman's handout. He did his walk. He longed for something, maybe the warmth of the house and the lights and the approach itself. He couldn't go in as he had because no one opened the door. He would need to smell it and peer inside, anyhow, because it had fallen apart. Now he turned toward that place, and climbed up on the deck from the corner post. He maneuvered around the broken limbs and twigs as if he had done it a hundred times and walked toward the garage. He poked only head through, saw that Lolly was watching him from her bed. He went on in, jumped to the cabinet. Her tail, hanging over the backside of the bed, thumped lightly on the floor. She nosed around a few times, going out and coming back. She yelped once. Zeno stayed where he was. When Lolly came in the final time, settled the bed down by going around in circles four or five times, lowered, and eventually slept, Zeno opened his eyes and watched her. He got into his bed then, and in a few minutes yawned, stretched out, slept.

The ice and mush left, but noise came and

stayed. Nights were quiet, but from early in the morning through the full day, saws buzzed and machines groaned and roared, and hammers struck, and boards creaked and broke. The town was being cleaned and repaired. Zeno's nature needed something peaceful and regular, something he controlled. Trucks parked in the alley. Men clambered up ladders and cut branches, let them fall and then snipped or hacked off twigs and limbs, stacking them up, filling trash cans and truck beds. It went on and on. Everywhere. Men were on the deck, and on the roof. Zeno went into the house, up to the bedroom where Wilma and Josh slept, and still the sound of nailing was sharp and intolerable. In the basement, too. He went down the alley a long way, to the creek where he had been before, and where Lolly had sometimes run. He knew that because he smelled hints of her.

Even there, along the bank, he could hear the busy, busy, busy, busyness of the town's clean-up, and he couldn't rest. He went home. He marched into the house through the open garage door but had to wait at the top of the stairs by the dining room. No one opened it. He meowed, harshly, though only the dogs heard. They knew something was up. The white cat was

120

wilder. He moved too quickly, he didn't sit and bathe, or even clean a paw. He went outside, looked at the men on the deck with such alarm in his face, like they were vicious animals and he was cornered. He scrambled over the gate post and to the front of the house onto the red bench and stared at the door. He meowed. He jumped down and rattled the screen door. He scratched at the wood rapidly, so fast the door quivered, yet he had never done that before. It may have been like crying. His body may have erupted with emotion. He turned his back to the door and hit it with his right hind foot so fast it was like a spasm had loosened from his muscles. It was a special ability, acquired in moments of emergency, not by will but by need.

Wilma heard that strange rapid-shot rattling and something clued her that it wasn't the workmen—it was more personal and more urgent. She came downstairs and heard the direction of the rattle. She opened the main door and a raw, scratchy meow reached her ears. Zeno was distressed and the tone was distress. Distress. She opened the door and he marched in. He walked to the sofa, turned to face her, wagged his tail rapidly while he kind of fast-stepped with his rear feet.

She knew what he was doing! She had never seen him do it, but she knew! He was spraying the sofa! He was marking his territory and looking at her the whole while!

"Zeno!" she screamed. "Bad cat! Bad cat!" She ran for him and he ran away. He ran into the kitchen and then through the study and then back into the living room and up the stairs. She went after him. She didn't intend to hurt him. She wasn't even really angry. Wilma was frustrated and disgusted. She didn't like actions such as spraying, however natural they were. And for him to do it right in front of her, deliberately! She had to catch him and put him outside. It wasn't as bad, maybe, as having a skunk spray in the house, but it was pretty bad. He was on her and Josh's bed, right in the center of the heavy comforter they had paid a good deal of money for. It was pretty, and fashionable, and warm.

"Zeno!" she yelled. "Don't you dare! Don't you dare!"

It was too late. Zeno was afraid and frustrated and had released the only weapon he had to say he was worth something. He had a right to something, and it was in this house, and in their presence. He had no other family.

He was also, of course, saying Help. Please help me.

Wilma knew this, too. She still wasn't angry but her energy left her. She was defeated. She couldn't help this poor little guy.

She sat down in a wide and tall, blue brocade chair. Vaguely she was grateful that Zeno hadn't sprayed the chair. She leaned back. He was on the bed still, watching her. Then he just jumped down and left the room. She wearily followed him. He got behind the sofa and made the hollow meow sounds she had heard before.

She didn't want the sofa ruined. She didn't want to frighten him more. But! She moved the sofa at an angle so he must pass by her to escape. When he clawed over the back, Wilma nimbly caught him in both arms. He didn't scratch her, though he struggled and in that action his claws made small scratches on her arms, through the cotton of her shirt. She held on. She grabbed her purse and went out to the car holding him fast. He had to have help and so did she. The vet had to tell her what to do. Today. Spraying in the house! Nasty act. She managed to get inside her car while holding him, and once she shut the door, she released him. He bolted over the seat into the back, meowed fiercely, came back, rubbed his head frantically against the passenger side window, then hunkered down and stared at the seat.

"I'm sorry, baby," she said, and truly was, "but you're getting worse. I can't handle you."

At the veterinarian's office, Wilma slipped out of the car, leaving Zeno inside. The doctor's assistant, a tall blonde young man who loved animals and especially cats, went out with a cat-carry. He wore gloves. He came back without the cat-carry, but with Zeno lying along one forearm, gently held there by the other gloved hand.

"He'll be all right," the young man said. "I'll just take him on back now, though. That's best." He disappeared through a door Wilma hadn't noted before. How, she wondered, could he carry Zeno so easily? Because Zeno was angry with her, she knew. Not with the young man. She could hear slight barking from the kennel. She felt terribly alone and terribly mean-hearted. Zeno was just a cat. A baby, despite his age. Like a baby to her. She felt she had failed him but she didn't know what to do. She pressed her lips tightly together and bowed her head, staring at her hands. But resist it as she would, she cried. When the vet's assistant called her, she sniffed, swallowed, and went into the examination room. She couldn't meet the vet's eyes at first. She explained about the construction, about it coming right after the ice storm. "He doesn't like his life disrupted. He's always been fearful and maybe neurotic, but now he's frantic. He's spraying in the house. I didn't even know he *could* spray. He's been neutered."

"A neutered cat can spray, Wilma, male or female. He's probably been doing it outside all along. Now he's reacting to changes. I'll give him a shot to calm him down. We'll examine him later. We don't want to agitate him more. If you don't mind leaving him overnight, we'll let him rest and give him a full look-over tomorrow."

"I don't think I should leave him. That's one of the things he's probably most afraid of. Coming here disturbs him so. I just wanted help. But now I think maybe leaving him would be the wrong thing to do. Give him a shot and I'll take him home."

"Let him rest here, Wilma. He'll just sleep. He'll be calmer when he wakes. We can call you so you can be here during the exam if you like."

"I want to take him home now," Wilma insisted. "Would you just give him a shot so he'll sleep, and I'll take him home and bring him back in the morning." She was teary again. "I don't want him to think I threw him away." Her voice cracked.

The veterinarian believed that this woman, this Wilma, was near to breaking herself, and probably needed some medication, too, but it wasn't his place to say so, and he didn't really trust his judgment about humans, just about animals. And truth be told, he was better with big animals, best with horses, and fair with dogs.

Wilma sat in the waiting room lobby while the vet and his assistant soothed Zeno with medication and low, male voices. They let Wilma take a cat-carry home with Zeno inside. She didn't really need it because he was sedated and already docile. At home, she put it down on the floor at one edge of the living room. She brought a soft yellow towel from the laundry room cupboard and, first easing Zeno's limp, slim body out, she placed the towel inside the cat-carry, and then gently lifted him inside and onto the towel. It seemed almost like he was dead and she became afraid of the thought. She loved him, truly. He was just a crazy cat, so strange. So needy and brave. She didn't know what to do.

"Sorry, Zeno," she said. "I really am."

She didn't feel like fixing dinner, but she did so anyhow. She roasted a chicken and when it was nearly done, she cooked potatoes, mashing them with butter and cream. She cooked peas with tiny pearl onions. She opened two cans of pears and put them in a blue bowl. She set the table prettily. Before Josh came home, she fixed the dog's dinner, dry dog food, with a little bit of canned food, a few green beans and slivers of chicken. None of the food was fattening. She wanted them to have a variety. She would want a variety if she were a dog.

In the cat-carry, Zeno was not totally asleep. His body was resting in a way. It didn't move much but his mind felt like it wanted to be fast, it wanted to be angry. He was dissatisfied, discontent, but unable to identify the why or to run from it. The problem had to be here. Here. This was what was wrong. That's all he knew. He had no way of correcting anything. He remembered the big gray cat who had been so comfortable. The world had been comfortable with that cat. And where was he? He had been in the garage. Then gone. Zeno lay still, his mind living places and events over and over, but shadowy, not complete, just bits of pictures and bits of emotions.

He smelled the warm scent of animals. Dogs. Dogs he knew. They nosed up to the cage. They knew him. He smelled a food he liked and ate often. He heard Wilma's voice and Josh's. He didn't make a sound until he needed to go outside. Then he meowed. Josh came into the room and carried the cat-carry upstairs to the bathroom where the kitty litter was. He closed the door and opened the cat-carry.

"You're in trouble fellow," Josh said. He rubbed Zeno's head sturdily. Zeno climbed into the litterbox like the well trained cat he could be and usually was.

Wilma dragged the big comforter down the stairs and to the garage, to take to the cleaner next day.

Zeno didn't fight being put back inside the cat-carry. He slept off and on during the night, in the bedroom with Wilma and Josh, but on the floor. He knew Speeds checked on him and so did Lolly. He wanted to be out with them or have them in the cat-carry with him. With him.

Zeno had to be given pills, the veterinarian said, at least for a while, to ease his body and mind down from the present desperate level.

Zeno was ready for them and equal to the task. He couldn't be fooled. He could smell a pill ground so fine it was dust and hidden in slivers of chicken. He could tell when Josh or Wilma had the pill on their person. Or maybe it was that he simply suspected pills all the time and immediately withdrew if he were touched differently. When Wilma finally developed a technique for giving him a pill, she felt herself to be an animal abuser, and made an appointment with the veterinarian to learn how to administer the medication better.

"He struggles so hard," she said. "He snaps his head and pushes and hisses. He's like a rope muscle. He can twist himself so! And saliva drips from his mouth. He gags, Dr. Will. He gags and he won't stop fighting me. I have found one way to do it, but it has to be quick and usually Josh has to help. The two of us. We don't want to keep this up. Would you please show us how to give him a pill?"

The tall veterinarian put the cat-carry on the metal table, opened the door, and extracted Zeno, who tensed, silently protested, pushing backward, not looking at Wilma or anyone, rescuing himself. With one hand, the doctor flipped off the plastic top of a pill container and tipped out one tiny white pill. As he set the container down on the table behind him, and took up the pill in his right hand, he grasped Zeno very firmly, too firmly, behind the shoulders, over that thin body, which was hunching now, squirming and scrawling flat and trying to wriggle away.

"Like this," Dr. Will said. His left hand pulled Zeno near swiftly, turning Zeno's back to the doctor, while his right came quickly to Zeno's mouth and pushed the tiny pill into the front, between the two fangs.

Zeno bit him and in the immediate release slashed out and caught with his claws the same hand he had bitten. The doctor released a sharp curse, and said, "Some cats can't be treated," while he opened a glass container and took out a square of wet gauze. He placed it over the bleeding lines on the back of his right hand. "He's one of them."

He wasn't speaking harshly. He managed not to look hurt or embarrassed. He was still placid and soft voiced. But Wilma had eyes for the white cat who had leapt from the table and was snaking back and forth at the bottom seam of the door, a door out to nowhere for that creature. Desperation filled Wilma, too. The moist pill lay before her. She moved it nearer. She took the towel from the cat-carry. "Let me show you," she said. Deftly and gently, she draped the towel over Zeno, lifted him swiftly and easily to the table and as she picked up the pill she tightened the towel just under his neck. She pushed the pill into the side of his mouth as he jerked away and slid thumb and index finger to clamp shut his mouth. She had him firm. As she released his mouth, she stroked the throat, urging the pill down. Saliva dripped from one edge of his mouth. Betrayed by everyone. An object.

"That's how Josh and I do it. Josh usually has the towel part." She put on her coat, picked up Zeno who struggled but didn't attack. He welcomed the cat-carry. She closed its metal grate and hated everything that had just happened.

"Wilma," the doctor said, "Zeno really is a tough cat to treat. If you can keep him medicated, you'll all be better off. There are other medications. They're a little more costly, but easier to give him."

"I don't know," she said. "Maybe we've never handled this right. But we're not going to give up. I should've left him alone just now. He'd had enough stress."

The doctor didn't disagree and Wilma felt doubly bad.

Zeno rested in the cat-carry which, in a way, was familiar, similar to the one he had been placed in as a kitten, the one swatted into the dark by the panther that had dumped him onto the ground. He had run through a garden and away. Now, he had been on medication for a while, had been given a new pill, and he was in a strange kind of uncomfortable peace, quietening down more quickly from the frenzy at the veterinarian's. He slept it seemed a long time, though it wasn't, and when Wilma took him out, he felt rather thick. His mouth still held dry bits of the pill and he wanted water. He wanted to be set free outside the house, but she took the cat-carry inside and released him there. He swayed while walking to the kitchen. He made it to the water dish. The water level was low, not freshened from the dogs' morning drinks. He would have preferred fresh, maybe, but then there's a comfort in a community water hole, a familial water hole. He lapped enough to rinse most of the pill residue down and then he went to the kitchen door and looked at the door knob. He smelled the seam of the door, then stretched to reach the door knob. He couldn't reach it. The door was old and the knob had been set higher a long time ago.

Wilma saw what he wanted. He wanted out. Now. Out. He didn't look at her. She went over as if she were going to open the door, but she lifted him instead. He tugged back but she crooned, "Oh Zeno, baby," and he eased into her hands and against her shoulder. Wilma held him the way she would hold a real baby, a tiny one, over her shoulder. "Won't you purr for me?" she said. "Just a little purr?"

He didn't, but he didn't pull away or ask to be put down. The soft tones were calming. He felt the reverberations of her voice in her throat and in his body. If she could have held him there without moving for a while, or at least made languid moves, with that rich rolling sweet sound, he might have slept there. And dreamed.

But something roused both of them, and he turned quickly and she released him in a gentle slide to the floor.

"Okay," she said. She opened the door for him, closed it, then watched through the door window.

He sat in the middle of the deck, bathing. Paws, face, chest. She went on with things that occupied her, paying some bills, unloading the dishwasher, bringing in the dogs and trying to withstand their exuberance.

Zeno, finished with his cleaning, still a little groggy, looked at the kitchen window. He wanted in again, but he didn't either. He might have to hide again, or jump on the bed. He remembered being yelled at, and chased, and leaping over the sofa, and going places with dogs and cats, being prodded and being caged. He thought of Wilma and felt two ways about her. So he wanted in and not in. Now, he got on the railing and surveyed the yard and neighbors' yards. He could see car lights on the road past the next house. Directly ahead, past the alley, the parking lot had many cars. He sometimes went under them and smelled tires with the traces of strange places.

He struck out, exiting the yard over the east gate post. He looked down to the other gate where he used to crawl through the dirt. He wanted to go back into the yard and leave that way, but didn't. He turned to his right, down the length of the fence. He heard Josh call from the deck and he stopped and glanced up.

"Hey fellow. Zeno! Want to come home?" Josh tapped the railing as if he had something for

Zeno. Zeno liked the tap. He liked the familiarity of the tap. He liked Josh. But he turned back to his walk, still not steady, not quite right. To the alley. Then to his left.

Zeno didn't plan not to enter the big house again. But when he came home and Wilma opened the door, he cautiously scanned the kitchen, to see what was in there, and who. He didn't have to live in there. He didn't have to get in the cat-carry. He didn't have to be chased or to get on the bed.

"Come on, Zeno," Wilma said. He backed away, as if she had made a move. Josh came to the door. "Hey Zeno!"

They left the door open for a while. Zeno crept close, stood on his hind legs, one paw on the screen, peering all around. But he stayed on the deck.

When the house shut down for the night, Wilma and Josh talked about letting him do just what he wanted.

"Let's put a small dog house on the deck," Josh said. "You don't want a cat window, but a little house would allow him shelter without even having to go in the garage, if he wanted."

"I wouldn't mind that. The cat window, though—I know you want one, but Josh, Zeno could spray everything in the house while we're gone. And something else could get in. A raccoon. Possum!"

"I know. I see your point. What about the little dog house?"

Wilma liked that idea. It was like a separate room for the white cat. Zeno.

Wilma put an old blanket in there, folded in fourths. The little house was blue, and it had a green shingled, one-ridge roof.

Zeno studied the house at night, when no one was around. He sniffed all the outer structure and the round entrance, poking his nose an inch inside. It smelled of new wood and something clinging, an oil scent. And the rag scent, which he associated with beds and cat-carries. He didn't enter then. The next morning he looked at it from the railing and Josh came out. Zeno left. Josh might put him inside the little structure.

"He's wary," Josh said.

When Zeno finally entered the dog house, he was very alert and couldn't give in to a true sleep. Something might creep over the gate, and onto the deck. He half-dozed.

Both Wilma and Josh checked the dog house a few times, but they didn't catch Zeno inside. One evening Josh brought in a little clump of fine white hair. "I scraped this off the bedding," he said. "He's sleeping there sometimes."

They felt very, very good. It was a step toward better, anyhow.

One time Zeno found the little house had been cleaned and turned east so the door faced out of the wind. Another time it had been turned to the north, toward the house. Zeno wouldn't enter it. The sudden cleanness was all right—towels and rags often disappeared and were returned clean—but a moving entrance was strange. Maybe dangerous. The house was one of his places, though, part of his home territory. So when the door faced the way Zeno preferred, he would sleep there if he wanted. If the dogs were in the yard while he slept, he felt totally guarded and protected. He came to believe, in his own way, that if a snarling face did appear in the opening to the little house, he could scratch it violently and drive it away. Being safe allowed him to sleep deeply and to believe he would be safe again.

Winter continued, but blessedly mild. Dark-eyed juncos, tufted titmouse, house wrens, waxwings, woodpeckers, cardinals, and kindred fowl visited neighborhood feeders and flickered and flew around bare branches and against a blue or gray or silver sky. The birds kept an eye on the white cat and occasionally swooped close as if to drive him away from their territory but only when he strayed into theirs. His lot was his lot. Theirs was theirs. He did hunt a little, as cats do, and now lived much of the time outdoors, though he ate often on the deck railing, where Josh and Wilma left food for him. Some days or nights when he felt the deep core need of something, he would rattle one of the house doors from the outside, and Wilma or Josh would gladly open it and offer him special food. He accepted attention from both Wilma and Josh, even rubbing against their legs. Purr for them. He would even sleep inside now and then, sleep so soundly by Josh or Wilma or Speeds, curled and silent. He was himself like a blessing in the house, like a wayfaring friend.

Speeds liked having him inside. She would preen a little, walk stiffly and proudly as if she had engineered his coming. And she relished his closeness, when he chose her for a nap. Lucky quietly enjoyed the visit with no responsibility on his part. The white cat was older, so was Lucky, and a proximity for years had bred some comfort between them. Lucky liked most of all that the cat was an independent. He survived free and went Lucky knew not where. Lolly nosed Zeno when he entered, followed him until he settled, but bore him no hard feelings. She liked him. If he had been a playing cat, she would have instigated teasing and tolerated it herself.

They were all at peace with Zeno being not totally of the fold. A little ache lived in the heart of each that the white cat wasn't really happy and braved worse lonesomeness than any of the others, but they couldn't do anything about it. His nature was his.

The Coming of Kittens

Zeno smelled the presence of the new cat before he saw him. A male. The scent trail was on the deck and, when Josh opened the main door, drifted also from the kitchen. Zeno jumped to the railing, hunkered down. Josh came out with a black kitten, not a baby but not too big. His coat was black, thick, coarse, but glistened. He looked shiny and clean. He would prove to be a frequent bather and groomer, neat, casual, and perhaps lazy by nature. Maybe Zeno recognized some of these traits already, but certainly he knew it was a male and here, on the deck. Josh set the kitten on the railing, but at the opposite end from Zeno. It made a slight bid to move toward Zeno, and Josh laughed. The sound was unpleasant to Zeno. Cats know laughter. It wasn't a laugh for Zeno, but for the kitten. Zeno looked toward the back yard—the path was clear for running.

Josh cupped up the kitten, and Zeno's gaze was locked on that closeness.

"He likes you, Zeno." Josh came near, with the black one in his arms. "He's your right-hand man."

Though Zeno was really interested in the smaller cat, he jumped from the deck, strolled away, demonstrating haughtiness and disdain and boredom, though he felt something entirely different. He sat at the base of a plum tree and looked at the deck. Josh was still there, with the kitten. It wasn't looking at Zeno now. It was moving underneath Josh's hand. Zeno studied it until Josh said, "We're going in, Zeno. Want to come?" Zeno's answer was to leap up on the fence, balancing over the dangerous triangles, and then leaping to the outside.

Zeno felt he must come to the deck often or the kitten would claim it, but he didn't want to stay. He wanted to walk often and far. Spring was everywhere. The trees bloomed, grass grew soft, the trees and skies sang. He wanted to visit the water place, Bear Creek, and the street behind the school, where a basset hound liked him through the fence. He sprayed the deck railing posts and ground posts. He also sprayed two limestones in the foundation, two spirea bushes and the side of the front step. The spray marks were not too evident for eyes such as Wilma's or Josh's but Zeno felt the young cat would know. This was supposed to be Zeno's place.

The black kitten didn't know, or if he did, he feigned ignorance and innocence as Zeno sometimes did, perhaps from a similar need or desire. He didn't appear bossy or servile. He was neither Alpha or Omega. He was lazy and talkative. He had to be aware of a tension between him and the white cat. Maybe he had to grow into understanding. He was still young. His place wasn't yet known. Josh and Wilma named him Twitch.

Zeno took short trips. When he came back and found the black kitten, Twitch, in the little house, on the newest bedding—a rag of blue blanket—Zeno lay on the railing directly across from the opening, staring down at the interloper. The stare did not make the black uncomfortable. At least, he did not leave. He did not sleep either. He pretended to sleep, but Zeno knew. He came down silently and crept close to the opening and smelled the kitten. Awake. Feigning. Zeno sat erect, front paws together between the hind paws. Night was falling, but slowly, as happens in the spring. Sounds were muted. The air was sweet and his memories were everywhere. He looked at the kitten. He could swat the tail. He could meow a complaint. He raised himself tall and thin, twisting a bit as if to appear vicious, but only for a second, recalling the ability. He fell back into his normal posture. He sniffed the kitten again. There was room inside the dog house for two. Zeno was drawn toward it, but he couldn't. He tensed with the desire to enter, to begin a friendship. He breathed through his open mouth. Then, he just spun around, as if an immediate chore had come to mind. He was off the deck, taking long strides. He made a kind of challenge meow to the night, and let the kitten have his bed. He was afraid of the kind of cat it might be and didn't know he had the power to help determine that.

Lucky ignored Twitch. Lolly asserted her status, and whuffed him away. But Speeds, old and determined to stay in charge, was again plagued by an affectionate feline. The black kitten stroked her, forever rubbing against her, those short, intense, this and that way rubs. He slept in her bed. He lolled over her toys, and at times even tried to eat her dog food. She wouldn't allow that. She would bark and bark and come closer and finally nudge the cat away. She would never hurt it. And why? Speeds had never had babies but she was likely by nature a mother, whether her responsibility was a human full grown, or a fledgling cat. She might have even been gentle with a squirrel, though she was never tested. Squirrels are quick and have teased dogs for centuries.

Zeno saw the fondness the black had for Speeds, and Zeno accepted it. He and the black were alike in that way. The fondness sprang from a cat knowledge they shared—maybe all cats share—about a dog like Speeds.

Zeno also saw that the black cat wanted to be a dog. When Josh sat on a bench in the back yard and tossed a ball, the black ran after it, never as quick as the dogs, but even if he were closest to the ball, he couldn't take it in his small mouth. The dogs had it always. Speeds didn't try, because Speeds had never played. But Lolly wanted it, and Lucky. And Twitch. Sometimes he would lie down next to the ball and wrap his cat body around it, even fall asleep there. Zeno smelled the ball and found it foul. He left it lie. This was new to Zeno, how persistent was the black for canine games.

The old shed had been torn down. And

that part of the alley no longer had dogs. Young people lived in many of the houses. They called to Zeno. He wouldn't let anyone pet him. Twitch came into the alley and watched Zeno walking his path. Twitch followed a little way, sat, followed, sat. He went back home. Walking was just too strenuous for his constitution. Zeno didn't want Twitch along, but he minded him less. Lazy.

Wilma made a little ball of wadded paper held together with a rubberband. She threw the ball on the kitchen floor and Twitch ran after it and got it in his mouth.

"Bring it here," she said, clucking lightly. "Bring it!"

He didn't obey. She took it away, tossed it again. He went after it. "Bring it. *Cluck*. Come on." He dropped it, sat.

Zeno, waiting under the table for Wilma to open the door, saw the ball and knew what Wilma wanted. He could have gotten the ball either time and have taken it to Wilma. He could have done it quickly and could do it now. But he didn't. Twitch finally got the idea. He took the flimsy paper ball up in his mouth and carried it to Wilma.

"Good boy," she said. "Good boy."

Zeno strolled to the door and looked at the door knob. He stretched up, reaching with his paw.

"I know," Wilma said. "My life is ruled by animals."

Zeno had lost a portion of his comfort to the black cat. When Zeno came inside, he smelled that younger animal on most of the furniture. Zeno didn't hate him or dislike him. The cat wasn't friend, wasn't enemy, was a presence but not a true bother. Zeno accepted the right of the cat to be there and ignored him except for occasional bland examinations, when he studied the other male through eyes that appeared glazed and near sleep. Every creature who observed Twitch understood fairly soon that Twitch couldn't or wouldn't run fast. His back legs turned inward, and his belly didn't diminish as he lost baby fat, but narrowed, hanging down and, when he moved quickly, swinging from side to side.

After dark one night, when Twitch remained outside in the mild summer weather, a raccoon came from neighbor's tree to roof and down to railing. Zeno heard it coming and vacated the deck, choosing a backyard bench where he was still very visible, but safely away. The big raccoon lumbered toward Twitch, then snarled and charged, much faster than seemed possible. Twitch jumped from the deck to the chinaberry tree trunk and scrambled desperately upward onto a branch that was at least horizontal. Twitch lay prone on it, his soft body overlapping on each side, his meow thin but insistent.   He scooted further forward, worsening the situation.

Zeno didn't leave, though he was sorely agitated. Hearing desperate cries of another creature alarms them all. Surely the whole creature neighborhood heard. But the humans Josh and Wilma didn't. Zeno stayed on the bench, lowering his body down, his paws out, his eyes almost closed, like a Sphinx lion, passive and serene. Zeno wasn't at ease. He wanted Twitch out of the tree, but wanting was all he could do. Waiting is a cat specialty.

Another sound came from a distance. Low thunder, no lightning. It increased, rolled closer. Silent lightning flashed. Zeno stayed where he was. Then wide-spaced rain began. The meow from Twitch in the deck tree increased in volume. Zeno leapt down from the bench, went over the gate, and quickly down the alley, fleeing threat and disaster and the sound of Twitch's fear.

Josh and Wilma heard the cries sometime in the early morning, between the ebb and flow

148

of rain. They coaxed him to come down, but he didn't move, just clung where he was and emitted another mournful meow. "Oh, baby," Wilma repeated. "Poor baby." Josh propped a board from the base of a rail post to the tree trunk so Twitch could cross the plank to safety. Twitch would only turn his head a smidgeon of an inch, obviously afraid anything sideways would make him fall.

"Don't you climb that tree," Wilma admonished Josh. "I don't want Twitch up there but I don't want you hurt."

When morning came, Wilma called for help, but neither firemen nor the animal-control man were allowed to climb the tree after a cat. The rescue couldn't be easily and safely effected, so the black cat had to come down on his own. And he did, but not for another day, when Twitch either fell or just let go in a kind of jump. As far as Wilma and Josh could tell, no part of him was hurt except cat dignity and he didn't seem concerned about that.

Zeno came home.

"Why didn't you get him down?" Wilma asked. She meant it in a small way, wondering if one cat could carry another to safety as mother cats did their kittens. But realistically, could thin Zeno have carried hefty Twitch? And would Twitch have let go of the bark? No to both. Twitch's own fear drove him up and kept him there.

In clear weather, when Twitch was in the yard, Zeno demonstrated postures, and how to fake run to a tree and swerve, or zip up it, stop short. How to back down quickly in a straight line or curving around the trunk. This Zeno could do, with grace and speed, without thought. His agility was such that his energy wasn't sapped. He was beautiful to watch, and Twitch did watch. He would lower his eyelids sleepily as if bored, but who knows what he was thinking and saying. Cats have complex intelligence and complex language. Zeno surely understood. Twitch couldn't learn the skills. He didn't have it in him.

The two males didn't groom one another but they often stayed in close proximity, as if one could be bored for the other, and the other could run for the one. Not friends. Same family. Accepting one another peacefully.

And then came another kitten.

Zeno knew of the new kitten's presence just as he had known of Twitch's. Outside, the weather warm and the neighborhood yard life full and bustling, he smelled her. The air seemed alive with her presence as though many creatures buzzed and their signals electrified the atmosphere. That might actually be true in some small degree, as everything in the world affects something else.

Her first two nights in the house, she meowed insistently, starting out with a gentle mew that eventually became a kind of raspy meow, a tired but young meow, complaining but not too loud. She may have slept for a while between bouts of complaining. The third night, Josh took her upstairs to their bedroom, brought the kitty-litter pan into the room, and let the kitten stay on the bed. Wilma approved. The kitten purred in their faces until she fell asleep, and again a couple hours later. When Josh woke in the morning, he found the kitten in the floor, asleep on a sock that might have come from the closet, partly ajar. When she realized he was awake, she tried to climb the bedspread. He thought it the cutest thing he'd seen, but he didn't want to be disloyal to Zeno, who as yet hadn't seen her.

Wilma took the kitten into the back yard the next morning. She had a cup of coffee with her and sat down on one of three benches grouped under the plum trees. Speeds was warily keeping her distance, but trembling. Maybe she couldn't quite see where the kitten was, not exactly. Speeds wanted to be by Wilma but not be treated too familiarly by the kitten. Lucky went into the garage. Lolly invited play by pouncing toward the kitten a little too boisterously. The kitten fired Lolly up. Life was faster with the kitten loose, and Lolly wished the gate would fly open—wished something like that, a freedom to run and get tangled in woods and splash through water and charge a squirrel or a rabbit and eat something strange. She nudged the kitten a bit too enthusiastically and Wilma took the little thing onto the deck and shut the stairway gate.

"You can't hold your own yet, foolish girl. Not yet."

The sun played so nicely in the kitten's fur, gray and white and kind of translucent. She seemed to glow, similar to Zeno in that way.

And where was that rascal?

Zeno had been under the neighbor's car in their back drive-through. He had seen that darting new kitten in his own yard. He had watched it avidly, unable to see enough, and had gone all the way around the house to come down on the east side, over the gate post close to the house, and under the deck. From there he had heard Twitch meowing in the kitchen, wanting out, and had had a long-shot view of the little female. He couldn't see enough of her, but he didn't want to get closer. He shivered with desire and dread simultaneously over the same object. If he could have expressed himself, he probably wanted the kitten to hold very still, perhaps to be asleep and everyone else gone or immobilized, so he could draw near enough to smell the kitten all over, even its ears and its breath, open his mouth and know it that special way, a closer scent drawn toward the back of his throat.

With Wilma and the kitten on the deck, Zeno peered upward, seeing the light and shadows of the kitten flitting across the deck boards, leaping, landing, rolling. Meowing. He listened to that, eyes looking at something only he saw, in his mind. Heard it, too. A memory. He broke his own restriction and went to the stairs. He leapt to the stair handrail, ran up it to the deck railing, and sat on the corner, openly and fixedly looking down at the creature.

"This is Pearly," Wilma said. "You treat her

nice."

Zeno heard the tone, but his eyes were on the kitten. It, Pearly, saw him. She wanted up where he was. She looked around, headed for the nearest post and climbed the length of her body plus three inches before half-tumbling, half backing up. She tried again. Wilma plucked her off the post and carried her gently but dangling in one hand and held her close to Zeno.

He swatted her.

He jumped down, ran fleetly to the back fence, up and over, to the parking lot.

The kitten was stunned, but only for seconds. Wilma was the devastated one. After all Zeno had suffered, after being loved and babied and protected to the best of her and Josh's ability, he had struck a baby kitten, something a fifth or sixth of his size.

She was so angry. And so guilty. Again. Had they made another mistake? A big one. Was everyone going to be miserable?

No. They weren't, though conflicts would arise. A trembling had begun in Zeno from an old want and an old love. For a family. He was so drawn to that little kitten that he was befuddled about what to do. It wasn't a romantic love in the sense of male and female. But it was a search in the sense of happiness and fulfillment. The kitten brought a change alive, a hope renewed, but Zeno didn't know that exactly. He just responded to it. He must do something. In the first instance of the power of the hope, he had slapped her. Well, not the best move, but not a terrible one. Cats slap each other with claws drawn in. It's a bit of a shock, but it initiates a relationship of sorts. Since he hit and ran, no harm intended.

The kitten was enthralled, but being so young, she was quickly involved in other matters—finding the litter box again; checking the food dish and rejecting it. The slap surely stayed in her memory, to surface when he came near, if he did.

Zeno went on his walking route, the most constant aspect of his life. His stride was longer and he held his head up. Some houses had been torn down, some new ones built. A high wooden fence blocked off the apartment house where students had once called to him, but two houses down was a little boy who would squat by the fence and call "Kitty." Zeno ignored him but he liked knowing he was there. Rabbits were in a high cage in a back yard farther on. No fence, but he shifted to the far side and walked in the rough slope up to an unkempt yard because the rabbit smell was unsettling. Perhaps because they were caged.

High on wires and in trees, birds who had seen him but not lived as long as others chirped warnings and swooped down but stopped because they weren't joined by others. A baby dove had fallen and was hiding in bent-over tall grass by a garbage bin. Zeno slowed and a dove flew low above him, wings audibly ruffling. Zeno went on. When he finished the longest route, he went back to the yard that was more his than any other place. He entered quietly, on a viewing mission.   From the garage roof nearest the deck stairs, if he leaned forward and peered right, into the kitchen window above the stove, he could see part of the refrigerator and the laundry upper-door. He couldn't of course see the floor or where the kitten was, but he repeatedly leaned out for a glimpse. Perhaps he could see shadows of movement or light or just knew from cat knowledge where the female was. After a while, he went down to the deck and sat by the door. He waited stoically for a long time, not bathing his paws, just listening more to the house than to the neighborhood. Then, with the claws of his right paw slightly exposed, he caught hold of the wooden frame of the screen door. He shook it, pulled it toward him and released it.

The woman, Wilma, opened the main door behind it.

He looked past her legs, seeking that kitten. He stood up, put his right paw on the screen and leaned in, peering this way and that, where he knew to look, and trying as well to look beyond, into the dining room. He didn't think about his inability to see around corners. He tried to see whatever was possible in the most direct way, and, failing, accepted and dropped his forepaws.

"You can come in, Zeno," Wilma said, holding the door agap enough for him to slide through, which he did, cautiously moving to the seat of a kitchen chair to look for the kitten. "But listen, Zeno. Zeno, are you listening? Be a good boy. A good boy."

There it was, the kitten, prancing in from somewhere, maybe from the secret recesses of the house, though wasn't it too tiny to go upstairs? It would have to struggle up each one whereas Zeno could thunderrun a zip up and a zip back. Zip. He'd show her. But he didn't move. She was prancing still. Aware of him? Surely. Cats are always aware of other cats. He turned as she moved around, watching her from the back of the chair, or from the front of another, slipping low and fast across the chair seats to keep her in view.

She hopped. Somersaulted.

"Cute, isn't she, Zeno? She reminds me of you, when you were a baby."

The kitten had found something very tiny, like a runt pea or a sliver of button and she knocked it around. Her moves were too agile, her paws too quick and coordinated for her to be a kitten. She hit the pea thing and it skittered to a rug by the study door. She was after the pea, pouncing on it, knocking it under the rug. Diving for it, rolling head over feet onto the rug, up three sideways jumps and jumps back and then to the rug, paws sliding under it, finding the pea, the hidden treasure. Zeno was wide awake. Zeno was poised to jump. Zeno was down on the floor.

"No, Zeno," Wilma said. "Leave her alone."

Zeno had no intention of doing otherwise. He leapt up to the chair again. When the kitten came over to the floor beneath him, he backed full onto the chair seat, lying flat, but hung his head over the edge.

The kitten stared at him. Her eyes were very round, blue, trusting, but also challenging though so young!

He had such longing that he bolted, ran upstairs, sought the litter box, and, without knowing what else to do, was ready to wet around it, on the floor, but Wilma was after him, upstairs, darting into the bathroom and lifting him up pretty gently.

"No you don't. Outside with you."

Saved from disaster. And didn't he know, poor old guy, poor white cat, carried downstairs, protesting mildly, outside, and set down on the railing. "Give her a chance," Wilma said. "Give yourself a chance."

Zeno hung around outside on the deck. Josh brought him chicken, tapped the railing. "Come on, fellow. Supper. Food, Zeno." Josh tapped and Zeno took a bite, another, backed up. Josh tapped again and again, then went on inside. Zeno tried to look through the window a couple of times. Twitch came home from wherever he had gone, somewhere down the street on the front side. Zeno didn't see awareness of the kitten in Twitch but there had to be. It wasn't the same with Twitch as it was with Zeno. Twitch stretched out on the floor of the deck, but Zeno moved to the railing by the house, nearest the laundry room window. He recalled sleeping on the other side of the window. Eating in there.

After a while, as the day heated and he was weary of the sun on his white-haired skin, he walked rather grandly to the benches under plum tree branches, where he took a half nap, opening his eyes at each movement of the dogs or Twitch and all the while looking for that cat. That kitten. Gray and white. He purred to himself now and then.

Cats purr even when alone, sometimes when ill, even when dying. Purring feels good to them. Comforting. They don't purr only when human hands stroke them. Listen to a mother cat with her babies. Oh, the roll of it. The sweet watery gentle sound of it. Love in sound. Touch in sound.

One morning Zeno was in the house early, when the kitten, Pearly, came into the kitchen, just having wakened from hours of sleep. Josh was at the table, having coffee. Wilma was leaning against the counter enumerating her planned activities. The sun was coming in through the east window and illuminated the kitten's fur, the purity of the white and the clean lines of the gray. She strolled across the yellow linoleum, stopped. She stretched slowly, lowering her forebody, raising rump up, placing one paw out and down, and then the other. A dramatic little stretch. So precise. So familiar.

Wilma looked from the kitten to Zeno, to Josh, to the kitten, to Zeno. "You know what?" she said. "She could be his sister. That was exactly Zeno's move, exactly the way he stretched when he was little."

"They all do it," Josh said.

"Nope. Not like that. It's different. I can tell. Twitch didn't do it."

"Probably takes too much effort."

They laughed.

"Besides," Josh continued, "she couldn't be his sister. He's much older."

"Related, though." Wilma wanted to believe they were alike in some ways. She wanted a bond among them all. So did Josh. So do most humans want to bond with their animal companions and seek ways of doing just that.

Zeno didn't know words like "sister" or "related" or "family," but his entire self knew the concept. He watched Pearly because he couldn't bear not to. He wanted her around, in the same space. He wouldn't touch her or share his food with her or lick one tip of one ear.

But his world had changed when that cat, that gray-white, fancy prancing kitten came into the house. He was rapt with anxiety and pleasure. So he came into the house more and more often. He would wait at the back door, go to the front, return to the back, and if no one opened either, he would rattle one. Rattle the door.

Zeno and Speeds sometimes lay together in the very middle of the yard, in a sun spot, her grizzled face and his white face pointed toward each other, legs toward one another. The breeze blew over them and Josh and Wilma would feel that they were living the best of lives, even with no children. Such wonderful creatures—the house always full of something funny or touching or loving.

Zeno was on the sofa back, lying in the slight dip of an afghan folded there, when Lolly was allowed in after an escape run. Chastised by Wilma, Lolly was unrepentant, no turning her head away, or slinking even a bit. She panted, threw herself down, then jerked up, moved a few inches, and threw herself down again. Burrs were tangled in her long hair. She sighed, much like a moan. Speeds growled at Lolly to be still, leave the shared space peaceful. Lolly struggled up once more, lay down crosswise in front of Lucky. He responded by scooting on his belly, as if in war time or on a dangerous savanna, low and steadily until his muzzle was touching Lolly. Then, as if he had done it a thousand times, he began to curry her fur. He took a small clump of hair in his teeth as if to chew it, but the chewing motions were tiny and start and stop. Thusly he worked the burrs out, one or two at a time, depositing them aside, so that a little pile grew. Josh, looking through a music catalog, stopped just to watch, and then called Wilma on his cell phone so she could come into the living room without his having to disturb this lovely process. Lucky stayed with Lolly, and when the time was right, she turned over and he moved around to the other side. He took out every burr. Josh took a couple of photos during the grooming and one of the amazing pile of burrs.

Zeno saw the interaction of dog to dog. He had seen cats groom one another, bathe another's shoulder or back or even face, gently over the closed eyes. Zeno had never been so bathed, except, perhaps, in another time, long ago, by a female cat, that was, and kittens. He understood what he saw. And he saw that Speeds was not part of it. She watched, her anxious nature feeling something he didn't know, and likely no one but Speeds could know. In Zeno's cat way, he sympathized. He, too, yearned for affection, yet could not be other than what he was. He could not accept every offering, no matter how well intended.

Pearly had a mean streak. Small, even as she grew quickly, she was more tightly muscled than either of the males in her life. Much quicker than Twitch. She teased everything, dogs, cats, Josh, Wilma. Sometimes, when they were petting her, she would let one claw pierce skin enough to hold on.

"You wicked thing!" Wilma would cry, or "Bad girl! Bad!" Even then, Pearly didn't cower or blink. She stared wide-eyed, as if saying *I'll do it again*.

Pearly liked the white cat. The humans knew it. She sought Zeno out the most to plague with her nature, spitting and hissing and, when he was peering down at her from a cushion or a railing or a bench, cavorting and tumbling and then lying very still, blinking slow and long in an invitation of peace and liking.

Zeno couldn't play. If he longed to, it didn't show in his outward demeanor, except in the intensity of his focus on her.

Twitch, who didn't cat-play either, would let Pearly have his food. He would lick the back of her neck and he would lie next to her for short naps—if she let him. True, she occasionally slapped him for no reason, which caused him to stay away till she was in a different frame of mind. But the presence of the female and her acceptance of him led Twitch astray. He became her accomplice, and Zeno's tormentor.

Zeno was going into the dining room when something nudged him roughly from behind, scooting him forward awkwardly. He spun, startled and feeling something like embarrassment. Twitch. Zeno showed his teeth, squirmed away backward enough that he could leap to a chair set near the piano. He gazed at the kitchen door frame, which was filled with morning light. Wilma was in the shower. The canines were outside. In the middle of the living room floor, still tiny and big eyed, was Pearly. Zeno was pinned to that room and chair. Behind him was a long, gauzy sheet of curtain. On top of the piano were small figurines of dwarf musicians, just obstacles to Zeno, that he would have to run over or past. Twitch moved and Zeno readied himself to leap on the piano, but Twitch strolled in his knock-kneed manner to Pearly, sat before her as if unaware she was present. Pearly kept her eyes tight on Zeno, unblinking. Thus Zeno understood—the two were working together. He couldn't get down until one of the humans came in the room. When Wilma appeared, Zeno meowed *out*, walking rapidly to the kitchen door, not running, but insisting *here*, at the yellow door to the outside. *Here*. And already Pearly was in the kitchen, behind, near the table, sitting as if inattentive and bored, but he knew. She was ready to pounce.

What had happened? He was on the deck, the other two were inside, and now that place was a hazard. It had been a good place. He went to the screen door and looked in, filled with the need to reenter, to assert himself, to be sleeping on the sofa or on a chair in the kitchen, or even upstairs where a window gave to the side yard. He saw Twitch had come up to Pearly, both of them now in the kitchen. Zeno stared hard, shivered his erect tail as if spraying at that very moment, owning the world. He didn't spray. All three of them probably had the same understanding, two were against one. Only one of them felt intense, familiar angst.

Zeno tried entering a few more times. He wasn't attacked harshly. No bites, no hissing. The bullying was so mild that for a while Josh and Wilma didn't see what was happening, though they noticed Zeno was behaving very strangely. He was absolutely crazy and paranoid, peering in the screen like a monster might lurk under the table. If he didn't dart away, Josh or Wilma would pick him up and bring him inside. Then Josh saw one of the crude rear attacks by Twitch and yelled, "Hey! What's this?" Both humans began to keep sharp lookout. Josh, from the supper table, happened to see Pearly hiding in the corner of the dining room and as Zeno came from behind the sofa and around the door frame, she sprang forward and swatted his nose.

Josh put Pearly and Twitch on the deck, tried to pet Zeno, but Zeno avoided the touch, cringing back like Josh smelled frightening. "Come on, fellow," Josh said.

Zeno wanted out the front door immediately. *Open this one. This one.* He paced. *This one.* Josh obeyed.

Zeno stopped asking into the house altogether. He peeked in when the door was open and ate from a dish outside. He joined Josh or Wilma on the benches and sat on the front stoop. He slept in the little house, or the garage, or the deep basement, or down the alley under an eave or in someone's cellar. In the daytime, in the yard, he displayed his skills as always, but neither Twitch nor Pearly could approach him. If they did, he stopped his movement, stared at them with what passed for disdain but everyone, all creatures, knew was his form of bravery. Alone bravery. He hadn't given up everything. He began to sit on the railing when Twitch and Pearly were on the deck. The two bullies didn't challenge him. Likely they had not intended the extent of his reaction. They had only wanted a good game. Zeno had never played games.

Wilma tried to whisper and baby-talk him inside. No. She tried to carry him from railing to kitchen. No. He squirmed and pushed off so hard that one claw pierced deeply and a quarter-size bruise spread under her skin.

Zeno was accustomed to loss, to leaving the home behind, and yet, and yet. It was his home. He wanted it.

Josh again broached the idea of a cat entrance from deck to laundry room. "We need two ways in. If Pearly and Twitch are in the garage, Zeno can come through the laundry room. If they're in the house, he can go into the garage and basement. He can escape any harassment they start. Maybe he'll start coming in again. Let's help him get over this crazy fear."

"I want to. I just don't want wild creatures coming in."

"They won't, Wilma. With the pets we have, the house is pretty safe for everyone except Zeno. Come on. Give in."

From down in the yard, Wilma studied the different entrances to the yard and to the house. She remembered Zeno, how he used to come through between gate and post, digging out the dirt a little. How vulnerable he had been. Face bare to danger on one side and bottom to danger on the other. She shook her head at the feeling of guilt, not bad guilt, just a twinge of regret that she hadn't been smarter, more farseeing. Well, live and learn, she thought. The cats needed more than one way into and out of the yard, and into and out of the house. She would want that if she were one of them.

There was much commotion again at Zeno's house, but no strangers, no workmen except Josh and Wilma. All the animals liked the activity and were part of it. They moved in the proximity of either Josh or Wilma and took baths or studied the universe while their humans worked. Just inside the front fence, near the corner of the deck, Josh and Wilma fashioned a spiral ladder of small platform steps. From the front yard, a sloping board was a runway to the upper steps and the deck. In the rear, slump blocks outside the fence allowed easy access to a board braced like a shelf along the fence top, beneath the plum tree. Above the little dog house on the deck, a cat entrance replaced the bottom pane of the laundry room window, with a ledge on the outside and inside. A cat had safe passage to the top of the dryer and onto the washer or simply to the floor.

In winter the dogs could come and go through doggy doors into the garage and basement. The cats could come and go in and out of the yard, onto the deck, into the laundry room, and, if Wilma could bear leaving the kitchen door open, on into the house proper.

A safe house in a good neighborhood.

It was a compromise necessary because of all the natures in one family.

To Zeno, the window was very suspicious, though he had seen it built. He had seen fat Twitch maneuver in and out, cumbersome, almost too big. Pearly flowed through. The two were owning the window by use. Zeno smelled the window late at night. One night he slept on the ledge. But he didn't spray it or the little blue house or the deck. One night he sat on the ledge when everyone was in bed and the house was dark. There was no snow, but the moisture in the ground had frozen. The moon was a slice of white, and the ice slivers in the ground glittered like other stars. Zeno sat on the ledge. He could smell night and winter, and traces of the animals. He yearned to be something other than alone. He nosed at the thin rubber flap shielding the entrance, pushed it inward, and eased inside. The warmth of the laundry room was too much, but he didn't retreat. He listened, the whole of the house around him, like a world in itself. He knew fairly well who was where and some of the inhabitants were very aware that he was now inside.

The water bowl was full and he spent a few minutes there. Behind him, the refrigerator clicked and hummed, a familiar sound and thus soothing. A trail of water drops across the floor meant one of the dogs had drunk recently. The drops would dry into pale circles. Zeno left no drop. Being a cat, his tongue scooped water up and back quickly and efficiently. The inner rooms lured him, but he resisted. The house was somehow strange. He had given this place up. His paws moved restlessly, as if he kneaded cloth. There was a bed upstairs where Josh and Wilma slept, and the gray and white cat, Pearly. Lucky was nearer. Just stepping forward should be easy. Zeno's feet were ready. But in a few more seconds, he whipped around, up to the dryer, to the window, out on the ledge. The whole night was better. The canopy of trees, sky, even the isolation. He sat there for a long while, then sought another place to sleep.

Sometimes Zeno forgot to eat. Sometimes he stayed far away and listened to the calls of Wilma or Josh. That was his house, the place with the plum trees and the other animals, but so was not being there his. A decision of the moment, based on need and desire.

Zeno didn't feel right. He closed his eyes to wait it out. He moved now and then a few inches away and closed his eyes again. He stood, not steady yet, and then began walking his route. He didn't walk fast, and his tail was not fully erect. It wavered from side to side. His eyes were cast down. No bird swooped him. No dog barked. He came to the house and the fence with ledge and gate and spirea bush but he walked on ground to the front, unable to leap. He hunkered there, under the red bench. Wilma saw him when she opened the door to send Lolly for the paper. Lolly never got out the door because Wilma saw Zeno, saw that something was wrong, and rushed to scoop up the white cat and carry him into the house and call the vet.

Zeno was thin and dehydrated and needed fluids and antibiotics and rest and loving care, just loving care, which he wouldn't allow.

When they brought him home, they tried shutting him in, but it didn't work. He sat by the kitchen door, then the closed laundry room door, and then the front door. He meowed, a kind of strident but plaintive meow, pain-filled. *Out. Out.*

Wilma complied. God bless that cat, she couldn't help it. She carried him into the laundry room. He was so thin and so fierce at her to let him down. She set him on the dryer.

"There you go," she said. "You have to get out by yourself." Before her lips finished the last word, Zeno was through the window and streaking away.

"You had to, Wilma," Josh comforted her.

"He can't be confined. It's let him go when he wants or it's medication for you both." He chuckled, though it wasn't really funny to either of them.

Wilma put fresh water in the deck bowl, spread a little shredded chicken in the saucer with dry cat food. "It's here," she called, "if something else doesn't get it first."

Zeno knew food would be on the deck. The chicken food. Water was always there. He blinked and half-slept beneath the plum tree, his beautiful green eyes opening a little now and then. Sick cat, but on the mend. Catbirds, cowbirds, finches, wrens, a mockingbird. Music came from down the alley and Zeno knew where that sound came from. He had visited the yard there. He heard a basset hound bayhoo. It had a name he had heard the humans call. Blossom. Her bayhoo sounded a little like that sound. BLOSSom. BLOSSSSSSommmmm.

Peace settled. Zeno kept his routes. Zeno came in when he wished, slinking around the edges of rooms. He was not attacked, but he didn't position himself to be attacked. He looked for clear passage. He talked with Wilma and Josh, his articulations short, barked meows, which Pearly spoke, too. They descended the same; leapt the same. Pearly mimicked his regal pose but she was short and round-muscled, feminine no matter how fierce she tried to be. When she slept, her tail curled, and often she would extend one arm and lay her head against it. Twitch acquired a similar posture, though he couldn't curl his tail. Zeno didn't mimic.

A Family Bond

Josh opened the dining room door to the garage. "Lucky," he called. "Come on. Bedtime." Lucky didn't come. "Lucky?" Josh heard a slight noise and flipped on the light. Feet away, near the south wall, Lucky lay. His body was arched stiffly but thrashing. "Lucky!"

Josh ran down the stairs. "Wilma!" he yelled. He knelt, saw the rolled back eyes, the rigidity. A seizure. "Wilma!" He slipped his forearms under Lucky, tried to lift and stand, but his legs buckled. He tried again and stood, stumbling toward the open rear door and his truck beyond, calling "Wilma!" She was behind him when he reached the gate. "Call the vet," he said. "Lucky's having a seizure."

Lucky had eaten something poisonous. On their afternoon walk, when he nosed always to the perimeter of the alley, nudging bits of trash, Lucky had found something, perhaps a thrown away packaging of poison used in a cleaned rental. Whatever the source, Lucky could not survive and be all right. His family, who loved him, let him go. They let the vet ease his way.

Zeno smelled the garage floor, sat by the doggy door. Leashes hung on the wall. He remembered Tristan. He slipped through the doggy door, up to the deck, looked at the window ledge. Someone was gone. Everyone could be gone. The house could be empty. He had memories of it empty. He jumped to the top of the little house, to the ledge, and poked the rubber flap of the window so he could smell the laundry room. Warm. He held his head there waiting for more clues, vulnerable with his white body so starkly visible to the outside world. He inched in, sat on the washer a while, then to the linoleum and into the kitchen. The water bowl.

He went on, stopped in the living room by the burgundy chair. Twitch lay on the back of the sofa. His eyes opened and closed, brief amber-green slits in the dimness.

The room was huge. The far wall held the staircase, but at the bottom landing was a narrow, vertical window. Zeno, looking up from across the room, could see the pale night sky and a brighter glow from a streetlight just out of view. At the very bottom of the stairs lay Speeds. Her breathing wasn't slow enough for deep sleep. Behind her was the old crock that held umbrellas. Alongside the staircase on the room side was a huge, square, flattish pillow, red and black plaid, where Speeds was now supposed to sleep. She was old, not so much for a small dog—she could live possibly to fifteen or more—but she was very stiff, a little deaf, and completely blind. She couldn't climb the stairs alone and needed to be on ground level, near water and food. Josh and Wilma had placed Speeds on the pillow a few times and had sat there with her. Speeds would have none of it. She rejected that pillow. She took her night's rest on the hard floor.

Pearly came down a few steps, peered at Zeno. Blinked slowly. Lay down.

Zeno felt so much, a twist of good and bad. Fear of having, fear of losing. Speeds made small moaning sounds now and then, like wistful snores. After a while, Zeno strolled across the milky night of the room and sat by the pillow. Then he walked onto it and sat in the very center. He moistened his paws and bathed his face and eyes. He knew Speeds was old, just as he had known that Pearly was a kitten and female. Maybe he knew Speeds' anguish at losing power, at her inability to meet the demands she had for herself. He lay down on his side, curled in a semi-circle with his tail drawn close. Soon he heard Speeds' breathing change, knew she was awake. Then he heard the rustle of her movement and the sound of claws on wood. A heaviness he could smell and identify and had actually been waiting on came to the pillow, and in a few more seconds, came onto it and settled down beside him. Speeds. He welcomed the familiar denseness of her canine body, the earthy scent. Good. He fell asleep after she did, so comfortable that the tip of his pink tongue showed between his lips.

Zeno's Walking

He walked so many seasons, so many years. He was often fearful, always brave, though he couldn't have known the latter. Admittedly, he did mark his territory now and then, and he branched out, his territory expanding, then retracting, with the ebbs and flows of his life. He much enjoyed Bear Creek and the density of the living fabric there. He nearly drowned once, falling into deeper water while terrified of something ferocious, possibly a fox or a coyote, though he scrambled away so quickly from the hot smell that he didn't get a good glimpse. He swam rapidly and smoothly and got out on the other side and shot through brambles—almost impossible to do—to the top of that bank and down along the upper flat of it until he paused, and then, not gasping but heart pounding so bad he shook, he sat and turned, his green eyes still somehow placid. Maybe he had learned to keep most feeling from expression because facial expression of fear had not served him well after the first few weeks of his life.

At Bear Creek, he had killed a snake. He had been wary of ropy things for a long time, but that wariness lessened and he had crossed over a snake who sliced at him immediately and he bit it the same instant, having no choice. He held fast as it thrashed so much he himself was dragged around. He wanted to let go but couldn't. His instinct told him, from the muscle thrust and the sheer power of the thing, that if he let go, he would suffer. Maybe he knew about death. Probably not. So he had a respect for all snakes, their strength and endurance. He had encountered skunks without consequence, and a runaway ferret, many owls and eagles. He shone at night like a fluid star.

Children often tried to coax him over. A little boy surprised him and grabbed him up and tried to drag him home. A little girl had a wooden spoon in one hand and tried to grab Zeno with the other. Another girl had a pink ribbon and a desire to decorate the white cat. Once he was stuck in a plastic car but bolted out the other window. He didn't like children. If he saw one, he stopped and found an alternative route.

Some people tried to give him food, but even if the smell enticed him, he didn't eat it. He sniffed at it, backed away as if it were tainted, and walked on. A three-legged tiny dog, new to the neighborhood, charged forward to the length of his chain and barked loudly, far deeper and fuller than his size warranted. Zeno studied the dog, seeing the difference in the body without judgment. Animals do feel compassion, but likely none was needed here. Zeno wasn't fearful of dogs, perhaps because of home and Speeds, but perhaps because he could out-maneuver them. They were usually chained and he could watch them if he wanted, stoically, or ignore them and explore. A group of young men caught him and carried him inside their house. They offered him milk and then a lid full of beer but he just protested and stayed by the door, meowing repeatedly, tail up, until they gladly released him. He was not a fun cat.

He endured some minor meannesses, inexplicable in human nature, and not worthy of reporting. All such experiences came inside him naturally, just as good things did. Zeno's life. No one knew the total of it. They saw only bits—his safeguards and determined boundaries. Walk this way. Walk that way. Always, though, he had

a home, the greater world, and then the littler
one. Spring with the cool nights and mornings
and the clearest air and skies and birdsong
and scents and the highest sky. Summer with
the burning stench of motors and rubber and
birthing and dying creatures, and left-over life
on banks and in garbage cans, and hot waves
of air lapping over ground and walks. Fall with
the mounds of whispers and whisking things, and
the coolish nights, and the ground crackly and
life withdrawing, covering, taking deep breaths
and waiting. Then the winter, high sky but cold
stars and sometimes he hurt with the snappish
wind and yet, how clean and pure. Eyesight
went so far then, and the air in lungs came
deep and forever. He shivered and may have
come near freezing but lived the moments to
the last and moved to shelter, under something,
in something. Rattled the door. Rattled the door.

Zeno was no coward. He had never given
up his sojourn into the world, no matter what lay
in wait. Let it come for him. He might run but he
came back. He even fought sometimes. He
had slashed and hissed and leapt and landed,
but he had not won so many as he had lost. He
wasn't mean enough. He could defend only,

184

and then when flight wasn't possible.

What a rich, rich, life they had, the whole troop of them.

Zeno. Ah, Zeno. Did he know that he was the Alpha Alpha? The old one even though he wasn't the oldest? Speeds and Lucky both had him beat in that regard. But he was an old soul. Whatever happened to him in those early days, the kitten days, fending for himself, with the help of other creatures in ways we can't know, made him solely his own. He struck out to make one more journey, gain another inch, sit on another wall, see another creature. He was fearful, yes, but did he let it drive him into a corner? No. He might rest in a corner, but he let his fear drive him into the world, to explore and be a survivor. He loved the world. Anyone could tell from the way he stared at the wind and the leaves and the birds and followed shadows. He might have been able to fly if he had lived long enough.

Josh and Wilma know they are going to have more companions, though they say "We can't take in more," or "it's too costly," or "they'll not all get along." A needy one will seek them out or they will stumble upon one who obviously needs their particular love. It's everywhere, that kind of love, some for this creature, or that one, or all of them. There's enough love, if only the opportunity comes at the right time—as Josh came that long ago day to Cave Hollow and Zeno ran straight to chance and hope. It was right and good. Now, Zeno is very, very old, and Josh and Wilma don't think of the day he won't be around anymore. He will always be there. Companions remain in the mind, and their features and actions arise in memory as vivid and precious as they had been in life. Possibly that's true in all the kingdom of living things, and the knowledge is passed down, so the mere presence of a creature enhances the beauty of the world for generations, at least generations, if not forever.

Other works by R.M. Kinder:

A Common Person and Other Stories,
University of Notre Dame,
Richard Sullivan Prize, 2021.

Universe Playing Strings,
University of New Mexico, 2016.

An Absolute Gentleman,
Counterpoint Press, 2007.

A Near-Perfect Gift: Stories,
University of Michigan,
Literary Fiction Award Series, 2005.

Sweet Angel Band & Other Stories,
Helicon 9, Willa Cather Award, 1991.